Fire Island Summer

Fire Island Summer

Julie Ellis

Five Star • Waterville, Maine

First Edition
Second Printing: August 2006

Published in 2006 in conjunction with Tekno Books.

Set in 11 pt. Plantin by Christina S. Huff.

Printed in the United States on permanent paper.

Library of Congress Cataloging-in-Publication Data

Ellis, Julie, 1933–
   Fire Island summer / Julie Ellis.—1st ed.
      p.   cm.
   ISBN 1-59414-474-5 (hc : alk. paper)
      1. Social workers—Fiction.   2. Fire Island (N.Y. : Island)—
Fiction.   I. Title.
   PS3555.L597F57 2006
   813´.54—dc22   2006005597

For Claire Gaynor and Charles Himmelman,
with whom I share fascinating memories.

Chapter One

On this last morning of the school year of 1992, Anne Evans sat at her desk in the Social Service Department of a South Bronx junior high school. Perspiration edged the mass of short dark hair that framed her delicately lovely face. For the moment—in tense conference with a student and mother— she was able to file away the triple-pronged personal hurdles to her peace of mind.

"I know you're goin' on vacation," Joey Devlin's mother apologized, her voice chronically over-loud. "But I just had to talk to you today about Joey."

"I don't go on vacation until three o'clock this afternoon, Mrs. Devlin," Anne said with an effort at humor. The "Mrs." was a matter of courtesy, which Anne doubted that Joey's mother appreciated. Twenty-seven-year-old Cora Devlin had been a hooker since Joey was three months old and his grandparents agreed to care for him. When his grandparents died in a fire five years ago, Cora had reluctantly taken Joey into her tiny tenement flat. Twelve-year-old Joey slept in one of two twin beds while his mother entertained clients in the other. His instructions were: *Pull the covers over your head and make like you're asleep.* "Joey knows I'm always available to both of you," Anne emphasized. "You're a family." But Cora's instincts were maternal on rare occasions.

Anne's blue eyes were troubled as she listened now to

Cora Devlin's belated maternal concern. In the next chair Joey fidgeted, struggling to hide his alarm beneath bravado. But Cora's reference to vacation had thrown Anne back into her own emotional turmoil.

Monday morning she would leave for Fire Island. Walking into the beach house would bring her face to face with the re- alization that her father and stepmother were dead. They had been killed in a smash-up on the Long Island Expressway last October after closing up the Fire Island house. Dad had died three years to the day after Sean's death in a hang-glider acci- dent. Sean and she had been married less than a year.

At the Fire Island house she would have to sort out Dad's belongings, the masses of clothes her stepmother had kept out there, and dispose of them. Already she felt the pain this would inflict on her. She should have rented the house for the summer—or put it up for sale, she reproached herself. Until now she had dodged facing this reality.

"Miss Evans, what are they gonna do to Joey?" Cora Devlin pulled her back to the interview.

"In a few weeks he'll come up before the judge in Family Court," Anne explained. "There'll be no jury. The records will be sealed. Since it's Joey's first offense, he may get off with probation."

Not so for the other two boys picked up with him, Anne thought grimly. At twelve—and looking fifteen—Perez and Smith had been in and out of Family Court for the past four years. But as every social worker and probation officer knew—and the kids as well—the reform school to which they'd be sent was only a revolving door. It was overcrowded and understaffed. In ninety days they'd be on the streets again.

"It's them dumb kids Joey hangs out with! That Luis Perez and Frank Smith," Cora flared. "They get him into trouble."

"Joey is responsible for his own actions, Mrs. Devlin."
Anne was firm. "Joey, you know the difference between right
and wrong." Chris, her boss, insisted that Perez and Smith
were sociopaths. Hostile to the world. They didn't know the
difference between right and wrong. Chris was ambivalent
about Joey.

"Miss Evans, I didn't do nothin'." Joey's Botticelli face re-
flected innocence. "I just went along with them."

"Joey, we know what happened. You were there. You
didn't try to stop them. You didn't walk away."

She couldn't believe that Joey was a sociopath. In the five
months that she had been seeing him regularly—after two
school-time scrapes—Joey had revealed a touching warmth
and a need for affection that convinced her he was salvage-
able.

In his early years he'd known loving grandparents, lived in
a small town upstate. Then he was thrown into the South
Bronx jungle. Right from their first encounter she'd realized
he'd displayed an artistic talent that was startling. That
hinted at a future that would take him out of the South
Bronx.

"I heard them two ten-year-old boys tell what happened."
Cora's face was grim. Mainly because this collision with the
law required time out of her own life. She turned her fury on
her son. "You cornered them two kids comin' out of that store,
luggin' the tent they'd just bought. You showed them a knife
and told them to return the tent and bring you the cash!"

"Not me!" Joey was defiant. "It was Luis and Frank."

"You were with them," Cora lashed back. "Them two
little kids were scared shitless. They did just what you told
them to." Anne guessed that their mothers had warned them
in the urban American tradition: "Don't argue with a
mugger. Give him what he wants." Cora turned to Anne.

9

"Excuse my French, Miss Evans—but I don't like my kid behavin' like trash." She turned back to Joey. "When them two boys came out with their money, you took it and then marched them over to that empty house off Lexington. You made them go inside and strip naked. You beat them up, set fire to their hair, and hung the littler one out the window, threatening to drop him—"

"Luis and Frank did it!" Joey yelled.

"And then you pushed them facedown on the floor and did it to them!" Cora was shaking. "What kinda son have I got?"

Joey flushed scarlet.

"Not me. *Them.*" Joey kept his eyes averted from Anne.

"If I catch you with them two creeps again, I'll burn your ass," Cora warned.

But out of this room Cora would forget. Joey would leave her to search out Perez and Smith. The odd trio from their neighborhood. Joey, small and appealing, the other two towering above him—swaggering in constant defiance. Anne was assaulted by the frustration she had encountered with painful frequency in the past two years that she had been a psychiatric social worker with the New York City school system. How could they change these kids unless they changed their lifestyles?

"You gonna be away for the whole summer, Miss Evans?" Joey found his voice again. Subdued, wistful.

"I'll be back when school opens in September," she said gently. Maybe she would be back. If she couldn't be effective on the job, she didn't want to stay in social work. She would have to wrestle with that problem this summer. "Joey, I can't help you if you don't try to help yourself." She flinched at the vision of Joey floating about the sweltering city streets all summer. With Perez and Smith.

"I'm gonna look for a job." Joey was shaken. A job at twelve? Anne asked herself. Running errands for small-time drug dealers? "I won't get in no more trouble." He hesitated. "Can I write to you, Miss Evans?" His eyes were a hopeful plea.

"Please do." Touched, she reached for a piece of paper and printed the post office box address on Fire Island. "Write to me, Joey."

Joey and Cora Devlin left Anne's office. Chris walked in with two containers of ice-islanded Cokes.

"This won't repair the air-conditioning, but it'll cool you a bit." Chris was an African-American who was phenomenally successful in handling troubled kids. Anne was grateful to be working with him.

"Thanks, Chris. I accept with pleasure."

"All geared for a summer at Fire Island?" He dropped himself into the chair recently vacated by Cora Devlin.

Anne sighed. "I don't know why I didn't arrange to rent the house for the summer. Or put it up for sale." The house was held in trust for her, didn't have to go through probate. To sell all she had to do was go to some county clerk's office with Dad's death certificate—the deed would be transferred to her name. Yet to do that emphasized her father's and step-mother's deaths.

"You were meant to spend a leisurely summer at the beach," Chris decided, radiating sympathy. "That would please your father."

"You'll come out for a week with Leona and the kids," Anne reminded. "You promised." In truth, she dreaded the prospect of being alone in the house.

"In August," Chris confirmed. "We're looking forward to it. Leona would divorce me we didn't go." His eyes were somber, belying his tone of raillery. "You're upset that your protégé's in trouble," he guessed. "What those little bastards did was sadistic."

"But Joey's different," she protested. "You said so yourself. And when you think of what Perez and Smith came out of—"

"Annie, you can't afford to get emotionally involved," Chris warned. "And don't tell me again how they're products of a violent society, and that we've got to feel for them!" Chris tapped inner springs of rage. "A twelve-year-old kid who commits a violent crime is as guilty as an adult. Don't blame it on the ghettos or TV or magazines. I came out of a Detroit ghetto. I never committed a crime."

"You had a decent family. Look what Joey and the other two come out of. I feel so helpless in dealing with these kids." She shook her head in frustration.

"Stop coddling them. As for Perez and Smith, they're classic sociopaths. They do terrible things and feel no remorse. See them as they are. Criminals. The world would be a better place if they could be put away for life."

"But not Joey Devlin." She was convinced Joey was different. "There's something good in Joey. And he's talented. You've seen his paintings. He could have a good life ahead—with help."

"Maybe Joey will straighten out," he conceded. "God knows, you're trying. But the other two—" He uttered a low sound of disgust. "They'll murder before they're through. And you'll see plenty more like them as long as you're sitting behind that desk in this school. Until we can make parents understand their obligations, we'll see kids like Perez and Smith messing up our school system."

Despite the sultry heat a coldness invaded Anne. Would she be back at her desk in the fall? She had a strange presentiment that this summer her whole life would change. And that was frightening . . .

Chapter Two

On a hot, late June Monday morning Mark Cameron emerged from the main building of the strung-out gray structures that made up the upstate New York prison complex, weighed down by two new valises bursting with the law and sociology books he'd acquired through the years. He wore the Brooks Brothers slacks and shirt, the Gucci loafers his mother had sent him for his reentry into society. The Brooks Brothers sports jacket was tossed over one shoulder.

Mark recalled with distaste the way he had come into this prison six years ago. Handcuffed. Ankles shackled. They had declared him dangerous because of his denunciation of the judge's sentence.

"I hereby sentence you to a term of twelve to eighteen years."

His presumably sharp, expensive attorney, who had talked about a sentence of two years—for a crime of which he was innocent—had bemoaned the heavy sentence with the eloquence of a Frankfurter or a Brandeis.

"But remember, Mark, the judge could have sentenced you to twenty-five years." He sighed. "Rough luck that we drew this judge. He's a great guy on the golf course or on some cut-and-dried lawsuit, but hell on wheels when it comes to rape."

Later Mark had learned that the judge's fifteen-year-old

daughter had been raped and murdered eleven years earlier. Nobody had been brought to trial. Rapists could expect the roughest sentence possible under law from this judge. He could understand the judge's feelings—but damn it, he wasn't a rapist!

A year after he was sent to prison, all that business about DNA testing began to hit the newspapers. The same year he'd gone to trial—1986—British police had approached a Dr. Alec Jeffreys at Leicester University and asked him to verify or deny a rape-murder suspect's confession. What Dr. Jeffreys had labeled "DNA fingerprints" proved the suspect was innocent. Every human being's DNA was different— with the sole exception of identical twins.

The next year—1987—in England a man named Robert Melias was the first suspect to be convicted of a crime on the strength of DNA evidence. And that, Mark remembered reading, had been a rape case. In November of that year a man named Tommy Lee Andrews was convicted of rape in Orange County, Florida, on the basis of DNA tests.

His timing was all wrong, he'd told himself a thousand times in painful frustration. The police didn't know about DNA tests when Lila Schrieber accused him of raping her. His DNA—his genetic imprint—wouldn't match the sperm found on Lila Schrieber's nightgown. But nobody knew about DNA testing when he was brought to trial.

In the last two years—right here in Suffolk County—two men were released from prison on these grounds. Mom had been wonderful—she'd gone out and hired a high-priced pair of lawyers to go to bat for him. But his case had been fully adjudicated—and no DNA evidence was available. Those other two guys were lucky—the DNA evidence was on file and properly stored.

Mark moved his tall, slim, muscular body towards the

main gate, set in the high wall that surrounded the prison. The guard reached to open the gate for him.

"It's hittin' ninety-eight out there today," the guard jibed, wiping perspiration from his face with a wad of tissues. "Sure you want to leave us today?"

"I come from rugged stock," Mark shot back with a grin. "I'll take a chance on surviving."

He crossed the threshold into freedom, paused and took a long breath. Savoring this moment. His eyes scanned the parking area. A sixtyish, shabbily dressed woman was approaching the entrance with poignant anticipation. Here, he guessed, to meet a released husband or son. Four of them were cutting out today.

Mom couldn't be here. For the past eight months she had been in South America with her new husband. He was on an engineering assignment down there. They'd be back in four months.

Mom had gone through hell with him. She treasured her summers at Fire Island, away from teaching in that rotten vocational high school. But she'd abandoned the beach house to stay with him in the Long Island house while he was out on bail. She hadn't missed a day in court.

His face tensed. Don't think about Dad. His father had been married to the corporate-executive rat race. Vowing to make it into top management. But the day never came. What about his sisters out in California? What did Barbara and Claire tell their kids about the uncle they'd never seen?

Mark spied an "I've been through the mill" eight-year-old green Plymouth pulling up at one side of the parking area. Chuck was behind the wheel. Grinning as though he was driving a late-model Porsche.

Chuck had bought the car, per Mark's instructions, with some of the money Mom had put into a joint checking account that was at his disposal. He knew he could trust Chuck with the money. Chuck looked forward to a payoff far beyond the cost of the tired old Plymouth. Far beyond anything he'd ever imagined. To Chuck it was as though he'd won a huge lottery ticket.

Bitterness charged through him. Chuck Ryan, a twenty-three-year-old ex-con, was his buddy. The friends he had anticipated collecting at Columbia Law School were forever denied him. His college buddies had drifted off into lives he couldn't share. He was an ex-con, a felon who didn't even have the right to vote.

In his short, hectic, slum-based life Chuck had been lucky in his skirmishes with the law. Only when he had "inherited" distribution rights to drugs on his corner in the South Bronx, when "his man" died of an OD, had he lost out to the fuzz. But Chuck, five weeks out of prison, was clean.

Chuck was "his man." He had sized Chuck up the first week they had been cellmates. Chuck would do anything that would be profitable for Chuck. He dreamt of owning a Porsche. Being a big wheel in his part of town. Flashing hundred-dollar bills to impress gorgeous chicks.

Chuck had been truant at school from the time he was nine, but he was gutter-sharp. Mark had dissected his brain, collecting knowledge that would be useful on the outside. In return Mark had spoon-fed Chuck with enough polish to play the role Mark intended for him to play. Not that much polish would be needed.

Short, wiry Chuck—flashily dressed—walked towards Mark with a broad grin. His eyes—which could range from ingenuous innocence to brutal ice—glowed with welcome.

"Hey, ya look pale, Attorney." He reached to take the valises from Mark—early on labeled "Attorney" in stir.

"You don't look as though you've been stretched out on

the beach." Mark relinquished one valise to Chuck.

Chuck made a clowning gesture of shock at the valise's weight. "You bringin' out gold bars?"

"The law library."

"I been workin' my ass off," Chuck confided as they walked towards the Plymouth. "I did everything just like you told me." Chuck had an astonishing collection of unsavory but useful "connections." Mark had rehearsed him endless hours on how to approach them. "Get in, Attorney." Chuck pulled open the door for him.

Chuck was gloating at this tie with him. Sure that he'd be led into the golden life. He had saved Chuck from a knifing their third week as cellmates. To both of them that seemed a mark of fate.

Chuck stowed the valises in the trunk. Mark settled himself in the car. His eyes dispassionately inspected the bleak, gray buildings behind the wall. Prison was his senior year of college, his graduate school. He had graduated *summa cum laude*. The warden's star boarder. The model prisoner paying his debt to society. A debt he had not owed.

Discipline had seen him through those years. That and the physical exercise he pushed upon himself. The home study courses. The long hours in the library, where he was able to read much of the time he was working there.

He had earned his college degree via correspondence courses. He took every correspondence course on law that was available. But even if he could get himself accepted at a law school now that he was on the outside, what was the point? A felon couldn't take the bar exams.

I'm taking the only road open to me. All the blueprints are laid out. We just need to follow them.

"I saw a great joint about a mile down where we can go in to eat," Chuck reported in high spirits. "It ain't a fancy

French restaurant, but it sure as hell beats slammer slop." He grinned. "I been eatin' like it was goin' outta style."

"We'll stop there," Mark agreed.

He was high on reality. He could eat any place he liked. Tonight he would sleep in a decent bed. No clanging of bars to shut him up for the night. No raucous night sounds. Tomorrow night when he stretched out to sleep in his bedroom in Mom's house on Fire Island, he'd hear only the beautiful sound of the surf pounding on the pristine shore.

They passed an Italian sports car driven by a striking blonde. For a moment Chuck's eyes left the road.

"Wow, would I love to plow into that!"

"Drive, you ape." But Mark chuckled. Sharing Chuck's exhilaration at being on the outside at last.

He leaned back in his seat. Assaulted by visions of a beachful of bikini-clad women—pretty, built, available. He closed his eyes, savoring in memory their sweet scent, their laughter, their appealing bodies. That had been one of the ugly realities of prison—no women.

Mark's face tightened as his mind zeroed in on what lay ahead for Chuck and him. They would make up for every rotten day they spent in prison. A sardonic smile touched his mouth. *The law provided them with the means.*

Mark tugged at the collar of his shirt. Perspiration trickled down his throat. The car's air-conditioning needed a repair job.

"It's hot," Chuck complained and fiddled—futilely—with the knobs on the air-conditioner.

"It'll be cool in the apartment," Mark comforted. "It has central air-conditioning."

Chuck uttered an anticipatory sigh. "I'll feel as though we've died and gone to heaven."

Tonight they'd sleep in the "junior four" apartment in the

West Seventies where Mom had moved when he went to prison. Now it was her co-op, available to him. "Tomorrow we'll be out on Fire Island."

Tomorrow night Chuck and he would walk along the night-deserted beach. Smell the ocean. Suddenly he couldn't wait to walk beside the ocean. God, he loved the surf, particularly when it was rough.

He had been staying for the summer at the beach house—which Dad was smug about having bought all those years ago before Fire Island property spiraled so insanely. With Dad's crazy working hours he and Mom wouldn't be out until the weekend. Mom always felt she had to stay at the apartment until Dad was free to go to the beach house.

That was the summer he was supposed to hitchhike through Europe again with Frank, then changed his mind. Why the hell hadn't he gone to Europe? Instead, he'd stayed on Fire Island—and all hell broke loose.

What was the name of that blonde he was having a thing with that summer? They both knew it was a summer-at-the-beach deal. Funny he couldn't remember her name.

She was older than he by at least seven years. All caught up in group sex, which turned him off. That night they'd had a few beers, gone to walk on the beach, made love under a blanket. Then she'd insisted on his going back to that crazy house where she was sharing—and he'd refused.

"You're a creep, you know?" she'd said with hostility when he refused to return with her.

She left him alone on the beach. He had stretched out on the cool white sand and stayed for at least an hour—gazing at the fog-shrouded sea until the cops showed.

"All right, on your feet." One of the cops prodded him with a foot because he was so relaxed he wasn't responding. "You've got some questions to answer."

Lila Schrieber's husband was a lawyer in the respected Manhattan firm of Carstairs, Schrieber, and Miller. When Schrieber walked into his house that night, Mark read later in the newspapers, he'd heard his wife screaming. He rushed inside to find her sprawled across the bed. Hysterical. Her nightgown torn. A window thrown open.

An attorney, Schreiber knew the score. No change of clothes, no shower, no douche. The courts would demand proof of rape. He hadn't allowed his wife to do more than throw a light coat over herself. He called the police and arranged for a boat to rush them—and a cop—to the Bay Shore hospital.

The doctor found semen to support her accusation of rape. Who the hell did rape Lila Schrieber? Why did she pick him out of the line-up the next morning? Weird.

He had not slept all that night. His head pounded from the unreality of the situation. Yet he had been convinced he would be released in the morning. He had denied, over and over, that he had been anywhere near Lila Schrieber's house, though it was only a few doors down from his own. He had been on the beach all evening, until they picked him up. No alibi to clear himself.

In the morning, he remembered with sharp recall, they had lined him up with five other guys. All about the same build. Same age. Same coloring. They'd flooded the six of them with lights. Then he heard that accusing voice—later identified as belonging to Lila Schrieber.

"That's the one. In jeans and blue sweatshirt!" The voice was strident. The accent reeking of bad diction lessons. "I told you he had a scar just above his wrist." The seven-inch scar he acquired at nine when he fell off his first two-wheeler. *How did she know that?*

"The restaurant's just ahead." Chuck punctured his introspection. He hesitated. "We're gonna be okay with money, Attorney?"

"We'll be all right till we set up our connections," Mark reassured him. Chuck knew this. He wanted reassurance. "You arranged the meeting with Brooks?"

"I handled it just like ya told me. All the way. Of course, it took a lotta doin'. A lotta followin' up on my old connections," Chuck bragged. "But I told you I could handle it." He cleared his throat nervously. "It's gonna work, Mark? Like you kept tellin' me in the slammer?"

"It'll work." For the last three years little else occupied his thoughts when he wasn't studying. He had ironed out every fine point. "The law hands us this deal on a silver platter. It's been there for grabs for years. Nobody spotted the potential. Chuck, we're going to see so much cash in our hands you'll shit green. And nobody," he said softly, *"nobody can touch us."*

Chapter Three

Sitting in a crowded car on the Long Island Rail Road en route to Bay Shore late Monday morning, Anne was tense with foreboding. But tension was laced with an unexpected relief as she sat in the taxi en route to the ferry. She was leaving the sultry heat of the city behind her. The endless city noises. The prospect of walking along a wide strip of sandy beach, with the salt air in her nostrils and the wind in her hair, was welcome. She was eager to board the ferry.

She was conscious of the familiar air of anticipation as passengers walked onto the ferry. Everyone relishing the escape from summer in Manhattan—or any of the five boroughs, she told herself. The atmosphere was convivial. She'd made this trip through her growing up years, the college years. But this time she traveled alone.

The small boat sped across the blue Atlantic. She relished the salt spray that grazed her face at intervals. The sky was a dramatic blue—not a cloud in sight. The atmosphere onboard that of a joyful escape.

The moment the island came into view she was swept up in anticipation. The noises of the city, the smells, the heat were behind her until September. No garbage truck would disturb her slumber at three in the morning. No need to pack herself into a crowded subway twice a day. No fears of violence in the school could haunt her. She hadn't even arranged to have the phone turned on. It would be peace and quiet all summer.

Now Joey intruded on her vision of a carefree summer. She had expected him to come back alone after her conference with him and his mother. That was his normal pattern. But he was embarrassed by his mother's frank description of what happened with those two little boys. Perez and Smith wouldn't have been embarrassed. What would happen to Joey this summer? Loose on the streets of the South Bronx.

The ferry pulled up at the dock. Passengers queued up to disembark. Impatient to begin their vacation lives. Conversations lively. The usual line-up of youngsters with wagons waiting to offer their services. No cars on the island. How great, Anne thought, not to be concerned about traffic, about drivers shooting through red lights, drivers who'd remained too long at a bar.

Anne hurried ashore. Immediately a small boy with a wagon came forward to take her luggage—in the long-established Fire Island tradition. He was like one of the middle-class private school kids whom Perez and Smith had faced in court yesterday. And Joey Devlin, she forced herself to acknowledge. Joey had been with Perez and Smith. He never denied that.

"I'd like to stop by the grocery for just a moment." She smiled at the eager little boy. Reminding herself that expensive private schools—in city and suburb—had problem students, too. Drugs and booze were not limited to Harlem and Bedford-Stuyvesant. "Okay?"

"Sure," he agreed and headed blithely for the grocery store.

Anne shopped for the few items she'd need to see her through dinner and tomorrow morning's breakfast. Tomorrow she would take her wagon and load up on supplies. Now she led the way to the house.

Her throat tightened as they approached their destination. Each weekend since early May she had planned to come out to tackle what had to be done. But coming to the house meant facing Dad's death. Mom had died when she was four. Dad was all she had. Both Mom and Dad had been only children—no siblings. The only family Anne had now were distant cousins living on the West Coast.

The Fire Island house had been built the summer of her seventh birthday. Seventeen years ago. She had adored spending summers here as a child. Waiting with Martha, their housekeeper, for Dad to arrive for the long weekends he took in the summer. But after Dad married Lila, she had spent little time at the house.

Her heart pounded as she turned into another lane. She knew the glass-fronted contemporary, its garden no doubt in desperate need of weeding, would be waiting for her a hundred feet ahead.

Here it was. Compulsively she sought for the marker at the edge of the path. *Shangri-La*. She leaned forward to uproot the marker, thrust it into a clump of bushes.

"Just leave the valises on the deck," she told the boy and shifted the groceries into one arm so that she could pull money from her purse.

"Sure thing." The little boy did as she instructed, accepted his financial reward with a broad grin and sprinted off after another customer.

Now Anne upbraided herself for coming out to the island. How could she endure spending a whole summer out here? Everywhere she looked she would encounter memories of Dad.

From the moment Dad married Lila, nine years ago, she'd

hated her. Not because she fought against accepting a step-mother. She knew Dad was lonely—he should remarry. But Lila was a calculating bitch.

She had loathed the way Lila used Dad. In the first year of their marriage she'd learned about Lila's afternoons at the cocktail lounges. About the nights—when Dad was away on behalf of some client—that Lila came home at four in the morning. Once she saw Lila emerge from a motel, arm in arm with a man. She had never told Dad. He thought he was in love with Lila.

Anne forced herself to walk into the house—expensively enlarged by Lila. Fighting tears she put away the groceries, plugged in the refrigerator. She had not arranged for phone service, she reminded herself—but no need for that. If something came up, she'd use the public phones in the village. Chris had her post office box number.

She hurried into her small, attractively furnished bedroom to change into a swimsuit, searched for an ankle-length terrycloth cover-up lest the sun was still high enough to burn, pulled down a floppy hat from the closet shelf. With her milk-white skin the sun was a formidable enemy. Dad had always warned her about the dangers of serious sunburns.

The house was oppressive with memories. The scent of Lila lingered in the rooms. It was wrong to think ill of the dead, she reproached herself—but she hated Lila.

She walked from the house, out into the fresh salt-scented air. The stairs to take her first up to an observation deck, then down to the beach, were close by. Headed for the stairs she smiled at a jaunty Irish setter dragging his mistress away from the beach. On the landing she paused to enjoy the view. The beach was nearly empty at this hour. The waves audaciously turbulent. The sky a dazzling blue.

The terrycloth cover-up billowing in the breeze, Anne

walked down the stairs—impatient for the feel of sand beneath her bare feet.

"Annie! Annie Evans!" A tall, well-preserved older woman with an air of commanding charm and lingering glamour beckoned to her. "Darling, I've been waiting for you to come out to the island. I've been here two weeks already."

"Doris—" Anne moved forward to embrace her with a surge of affection. How excited she had been, as a little girl, to find that their house on Fire Island was next to that of a Broadway actress. Her awe had spiraled when Doris confided she was seen regularly on a soap that Martha stopped work to watch every afternoon. "You're looking wonderful." Doris was part of her childhood. Never too busy to talk with her. To provide cookies or a sandwich. To treat her with delicious seriousness.

"Annie, I can't tell you how shocked and grieved I was to hear about your father. He was a beautiful man."

"I can't believe he's gone." Anne fought back tears. Doris was one of Dad's favorite people, though Lila was apt to make snide remarks about actresses in general and Doris in particular. "I keep expecting to turn around and see him coming up to the house. You know how he loved it out here."

Doris's eyes went opaque.

"Not so much these last years," she said with her usual candor. "Oh, he loved the island," she conceded, "but Lila gave him a devil of a time."

"I know." Anne lowered her eyes in discomfort.

"Remember, darling," Doris cautioned with a brilliant smile that was meant to dismiss the heaviness that swamped them, "lock your doors at night. Not that anything's happened since that awful incident with Lila, but everybody still leans over backwards to be cautious."

She had been working on a Navajo reservation that

summer, Anne recalled. She had not come out here at all. She had gone directly to college from the reservation. When she came home for Christmas, Lila had been full of talk about the trial. Alone with her one night when Dad was tied up with a client, Lila—on her fourth cocktail—had gone into clinical details.

"Annie, you wouldn't believe what they put me through. I knew what the charges entailed, of course. I wanted to drop them. Your father wouldn't hear of it. He said he would get a conviction of the bastard or die. You should have been in the hospital examining room with me that night. There I was on the table in a damn paper gown. My feet up in the stirrups so the doctor can take a vaginal smear. And this damn cop walks right into the room! Can you believe that? When I complained, he says he's here to be a witness for me!"

Anne shivered in distaste. So much about Lila turned her off.

"Of course," Doris picked up, jolting Anne back into the present, "Lila invited that sort of thing. I was a Lila-watcher. I knew—" Doris reached for a bottle of oil, concentrated on smoothing the liquid fragrance about her tanned face. "I'm really too old for this scene. I should be hiding my face under an umbrella, protecting the natural oils."

"Doris, you'll always be beautiful." Affection surged through Anne.

"Sure," Doris drawled. "Dragging my wrinkles around on wheels. Get a lot of sleep out here, love." Her eyes were compassionate. "You look as though you could use a lot of rest."

"I'm tired," Anne admitted.

"Sleep now," Doris commanded. "And cover your face with your hat. That sun's deceptive, low as it is."

Anne sprawled prone upon the sand. The terrycloth

cover-up protected her from neck to toe. She dropped the floppy hat across her face. Utilitarian and unglamorous.

The scent of the sea and the sound of the surf lulled her into restfulness. Here, she swore to herself, she would put the school behind her for the summer. Ignore the doubts that tugged at her. Could she make a difference with the school's troubled kids? Chris thought she could—

So Perez and Smith would be sent to a reform school— they'd be out on the street again in ninety days. The places were overcrowded. Only the worst of the very youthful offenders—guilty of murder—would be held. Chris was sure Joey would get off with probation. Would that be enough to shock him into good behavior?

The magic of the sea, churning with its special music, lulled her into semi-sleep. She was comforted, too, by Doris's silent presence.

" 'Bye, sweetie," Doris said softly after a while. Not sure if Anne was awake or drowsing.

Anne opened her eyes and smiled.

"Come over and have dinner with me some night," she invited and Doris laughed.

"I'm not the cookie lady anymore. God, that shows my age. Let's have dinner Thursday. At my place," Doris stipulated. "Lobster and a salad. I'm great at that."

Chapter Four

Mark came awake with a start. The alarm clock was screeching its message. With a grunt of protest, he reached out to silence it. At the same time, he was conscious of the pleasant air-conditioning. Now he glanced at the clock. It was 8:00 a.m. sharp. It had been a long time since he'd slept this late.

He and Chuck would take things easy for a couple of days—then they'd move into action. Chuck had made the essential connections. They'd meet with Mr. Brooks—as he preferred to be called—on schedule. That was arranged. Now they must focus on bringing together their team.

He lay back against the pillows for a luxurious few minutes. Lying here in Mom's bed, he felt her presence. He knew she'd be upset, fearful, if she guessed the road he planned to take. But his choices were extremely limited.

"Chuck," he called out. "Rise and shine." Chuck slept on a twin bed in the minuscule second bedroom of the "junior four"—meant to be at his own disposal any time he chose.

"Hey, it's daybreak," Chuck grumbled. "I been sleepin' till ten." In a stall-like room in a single occupancy hotel only blocks from here.

"We've got work to do," Mark reminded him and grinned. Chuck was out of bed and heading for the shower.

They showered, dressed, and headed downstairs to pick up the car. Mark had no driver's license. Chuck had acquired one on the street.

"We'll stop for breakfast out on the road," Mark decided, anxious to put the city behind him.

"You're the boss, Attorney." Chuck was ebullient this morning.

They drove downtown and across to the Queens Midtown Tunnel. Mark was conscious of the newness of the city after six years in prison.

"We're gonna run into heavy traffic on the expressway," Chuck warned as he maneuvered through the clogged Manhattan streets. "Everybody's runnin' to the beach in this weather."

Mark mentally plotted their day. The first stop would be Hempstead. He had to check in with his parole officer. He had been clued in to the fact that parole stations on Long Island were few. He'd have to come in once a month rather than weekly, as he would in the city. Being on Fire Island for the summer gave him this fringe benefit.

They inched their way through the tunnel. Mark was claustrophobic at this feeling of enclosure. Too much like prison. He was relieved when they emerged and moved onto the Long Island Expressway. His eyes swept the sun-drenched silhouette of Long Island City. The freight yards and the industrial buildings were an oppressive view.

Mark was silent as they headed out on the island. Damn it, why did they have that crazy rule about registering with the parole officer within twenty-four hours?

"You starving?" he asked Chuck. He was reluctant to stop before they were well out of the urban sprawl.

"I can wait." Chuck leaned forward to switch on the radio to a raucous loudness.

"Wait in lower tones," Mark reproached. Chuck lowered the volume.

Twenty minutes later Mark directed Chuck off the LIE. He had spied a diner. It was still a pleasure to realize that he could make these decisions.

They parked and went into a glittering blue-and-chrome diner. A radio blared out the morning news. Conservative Republicans were condemning the "liberal media."

They settled themselves in a booth that provided privacy. Mark ordered juice, a western omelet, and coffee. With an awareness of the money in his pocket and more to come, Chuck ordered steak, French fries, and beer.

Sipping freshly squeezed juice—an epicurean delight after the prison variety—Mark listened while Chuck outlined arrangements for their meeting at the plush Long Island estate of a big-time mobster. He paraded locally under the name of Brooks.

While Chuck talked, Mark's mind traitorously detoured to his last summer on the island. He relived the shock, the disbelief, the anger of those moments in the police line-up. Face to face with Lila Schrieber, he had recognized her.

Lila Schrieber lived in a cedar-and-glass contemporary that faced the ocean. Just the previous afternoon he had encountered her on the beach. Still attractive in a bikini, though he tagged her for early forties, she had made a blunt pitch for him.

With twenty-year-old arrogance—because he was startled—he had drawled, "Sorry, lady, you can't have my body." Wow, she was pissed. But enough to frame him on a rape charge? That he could never figure.

Segments of the trial flashed through his mind. The prosecuting attorney, so confident. He would prove three points, he told the jury: identification, penetration, and lack of consent.

Lila Schrieber identified him. The fact that she was the wife of a respected attorney and active in Westchester charities had been a blow to the defense. The hospital records corroborated penetration. Schrieber said he heard his wife screaming, "No! Please don't!" as he hurried into the house, his progress impeded by a recent leg injury. There was the lack of consent.

Lila Schrieber sat on the witness stand in a lilac pantsuit, her makeup dramatically subdued. She made a great witness for the prosecution.

"Mrs. Schrieber, I apologize for these questions, but it's necessary at this point. Did you consent to having sexual intercourse with the defendant?"

"I did not."

"Did you make any effort to fend him off?"

"I pleaded with him. I didn't dare do more. He held a knife at my throat."

Fremont—his overpriced attorney—knew they didn't have a chance. All he cared about was getting a lenient judge on the bench. But that hadn't happened.

One paunchy guy on the jury kept staring at him through the trial as though he'd enjoy castrating him. He heard later that only a black schoolteacher on the jury had held out against conviction. She had held out until the others had eroded her belief in his innocence.

Mark and Chuck left the diner, headed south towards Hempstead. Mark geared himself for the encounter at the parole office. While Chuck waited out front in the car, he went through the routine of registering with the Hempstead parole officer. He was polite and respectful. More quickly than he had anticipated, he was walking back to the car.

"They do things classy out here," Chuck drawled, reaching for the ignition key. "It ain't like in the South Bronx."

"We'll go out on the Sunrise Highway," Mark instructed. "Drive till I tell you to cut off."

He guided Chuck onto the Sunrise. Tension tightened the muscles at his shoulder blades. Soon they'd be in the community where he had lived with his family since he was two.

"Chuck, no tickets," Mark cautioned as Chuck weaved in and out of lanes. "We have to keep a low profile." They couldn't afford one careless move. Everything must be according to the book.

His eyes focused on the passing scenery. He had never been conscious of a need for luxury before going to prison. He had been into the public service options open to the law school graduate. Dad was impatient with that approach. It wasn't the late 'eighties scene.

"Mark, where's your ambition? When you come out of law school, don't throw away that education. It's an expensive investment!"

Like so many others, Dad was convinced happiness came with income tax problems. He didn't want the kinds of pressures Dad lived under. He had known what he wanted to do with his life—to be a lawyer defending the poor, fighting to make this a better world. But the law had taken away that right. A felon could not become a lawyer.

Mark and Chuck rode in silence for a while, into the flat greenness that was Long Island suburbia.

"Chuck, cut off at the next exit," Mark said on impulse. "I'll show you where I grew up."

"Sure, Attorney."

To Chuck home was a converted cold-water flat in the South Bronx. Chuck had talked about his life with disarming matter-of-factness. His growing-up summers had been spent sleeping on fire escapes, opening hydrants, running errands for small-time hoods who operated in the neighborhood.

Chuck cursed as a Honda cut across three lanes, almost causing a collision.

"I wish I had steel fenders! I'd ram the bastard!"

Mark leaned forward, shrouded in recall.

"Make a left here," he ordered as they emerged from the exit. "Two blocks down take a right."

A vein throbbed in his throat as he inspected the avenue of upper-middle-class houses that rose into view. Mom did well in selling, but she would have cleaned up if she had waited. But she couldn't bear to live out here after the trial.

The neighbors were convinced he was guilty. He had grown up in this neighborhood. Shared their lives. But he'd sprouted a beard and worn his hair long. He was playing the 'sixties scene in the 'eighties.

Would Lila Schrieber, with her frosted hair and designer clothes, be out on the island this summer? He'd enjoy walking up to her and spitting in her face. Yet he hoped simultaneously that the Schriebers had sold and moved on to the Hamptons.

Here and there children splashed in outdoor pools beside split-levels and mock colonials. Most of those residents with income tax bills large enough to hurt were out on the sundry beaches of Fire Island or the Hamptons.

Tension clamped a hold on the back of Mark's neck. They were approaching the tall white colonial that had been home for eighteen years. Mom had been so proud that the mortgage was down to the bottom. But they had refinanced the house to pay for his high-priced, ineffectual defense.

"Pull over to the curb, Chuck." His voice sounded unnatural to him. He leaned forward to peer past Chuck. "See that white house on the corner? That's where I used to live."

Chuck stared avidly.

"Jesus Christ! How many rooms in that convention hall?"

"Ten." It was the choice house in their section of custom houses. "Everybody had his own bedroom." Chuck had shared a bedroom with his brother, a sister, his grandmother, and a transient population of rats and roaches.

Mark's throat tightened as his eyes rested on the upstairs corner bedroom. His parents' room. In that room Dad had put a bullet through his head. Lila Schrieber had murdered his father.

Hadn't Dad realized what he was doing to *him?* Mom said he shot himself because he couldn't face his business associates. Had Dad believed he was guilty? He'd never know. Dad could have survived fraud. Even a drug charge, Mark thought bitterly. But rape was obscene.

Mom was stunned when the jury brought in the verdict. Right away she wanted to fight for an appeal. Fremont insisted they didn't have a chance. Then came the DNA news and she'd paid for a lot of billing by those two attorneys— which came to nothing.

Mom wrote regularly, visited him twice a month until her new husband was sent to South America on assignment. She mailed money and packages to him as though he was in the army or the Peace Corps. She kept a joint checking account and savings account in a Long Island bank, to be accessible to him when he was released.

"I want you to rest up this summer," she had written from Rio. Where did she expect him to get a job with his record? Slinging hamburgers at McDonald's? "I didn't rent out the house this summer."

At first he had recoiled from going out to Fire Island for the summer. But Mom remembered how much he loved the beach. Not even six years in prison could change that.

"Nobody will recognize you, Mark," she wrote.

That summer he was a skinny, bearded, intense twenty-year-old. Now he was clean-shaven, six years older, and fifteen pounds heavier. A man.

"Chuck, let's split."

He would give himself two days to lie around on the beach. Then he'd settle down to business. Not that he'd be overworking even then, he thought with ironic humor. Just using his brains to his greatest advantage.

After the first year in jail he had known he was a survivor. That first year—avoiding the bullies, the homosexual pitches, playing the model prisoner through clenched teeth because that was the road to early release—he had forged himself into a personality.

The other prisoners developed a reluctant respect for him. They didn't know they were his guinea pigs. He read everything he could lay his hands on about criminology. About the sociopathic mind.

At Bay Shore they left the car in a garage and took a taxi to the ferry. There was a twenty-five-minute wait for the next boat.

"Let's go for a cold drink," Mark said. "Why sit here and broil?"

"I ain't never been on a boat, ya know?" Chuck was self-conscious. "Except for the Staten Island Ferry once—and once on the Circle Line when a bunch of old biddies took some kids on a day trip." He grinned reminiscently. "When he was a kid, my old man used to work on one of them boats that went up the Hudson. Not on the day boat. The one that ran overnight. The day boat, he said, was run like a prayer meetin'. The night boat was a floatin' whorehouse."

All at once restlessness ripped at Mark. He couldn't wait to be standing on the deck of the ferry. To feel the wind blowing against his face. The salt spray rising to brush him with wetness. How many times, lying in his sweat-drenched prison bunk, had he thought about this short haul to Fire Island?

Mark and Chuck sat at a counter and swigged Cokes until it was time to board the ferry. Chuck was talking now about the trip he'd make up to his old turf. School was out in the city, he pointed out. It would be like picking off deer in a preserve to round up the kids they needed for this caper. None over twelve. *They had to be sure about the ages.*

"Jesus Christ, you're smart, Attorney," Chuck grinned in satisfaction. "I thought you was plannin' some jewelry heist with them kids. Nobody'll believe what you got lined up!"

Standing on the deck as the boat pulled away from shore, Mark was swept into the past. He remembered the parade of summers when Mom had transported the household to the house. Ranting religiously about the exorbitant prices in the local grocery stores. Dad coming out on weekends—dragging insulated bags loaded with steaks, chops, and delicatessen.

Only on Fire Island weekends did the Cameron children see much of their father. The rest of the year he was constantly involved with business. He played golf with the boss on weekends because that was the way to make it into top management. How many times a week did Dad sit down to dinner with them? There was always some business demand on his time.

Fire Island was the place where he could unwind from school pressures, Mark remembered. Swim. Overeat. Lie around with a book. The summer he was fourteen was spent reading everything he could find on Ralph Nader.

The next summer—hoping he'd make it into Columbia— he had been into a recall of the campus rebellion scene. James Simon Kunen and Dotson Rader were his heroes. He had been out of his mind with pleasure when his SAT scores were high enough to get him into Columbia.

"Hey, we're comin' to land," Chuck broke into his reverie. "Look!" He leaned forward to drink in their approach to shore.

All at once unease infiltrated Mark. Was he making a horrible mistake to come back to Fire Island? To spend the summer just eight houses away from the beachfront showplace that belonged to the Schriebers?

Maybe they had sold. Maybe they hadn't sold.

Don't be an ass. Why should I allow the memory of Lila Schrieber to spoil my whole summer? I'm dying to spend some time out here. And it's the perfect setup. An ideal base of operations.

Mark Cameron has been laid to rest. Mark Forrest is arriving to take over a beach rental. Mom rented out the house for the past five seasons. Nobody will recognize me. Nobody will remember the case. That's six-year-old news.

Chapter Five

After a night of broken sleep, Anne awoke with startling suddenness. No alarm clock this morning. The sun poured in through a chink in the drapes to blast her awake. The sound of the waves hitting the shore was pleasing evidence that she was far removed from the steaming streets of Manhattan.

She lay back against the pillows and planned the day. She would dress and hurry down to the stores before they became glutted with people. Then she must go through the closets and drawers, empty out their contents. God, she dreaded that! It would be a reaffirmation that her father would never again walk up the path to the house he had loved.

This was a summer when she must come to terms with her life. She had avoided any emotional involvement since Sean's death on that windy October afternoon three years ago. She had told herself she could survive without a man in her life. The job would be sufficient.

Now questions plagued her. She had wanted to go into social work since she was fourteen. She had such a longing to be useful. But if she couldn't help kids like Joey, then what was the point of staying in the field?

It was frightening to face the prospect of walking out of her job. What would she do with her life? There had to be a reason for being. A smile touched her mouth. Dad had an unswervable conviction that if something was meant to happen, it *would* happen.

The day moved ahead with painful slowness. By six o'clock Anne declared her work done for the day. Only then did she allow herself to go down to the beach. She pulled on a cover-up, decided to leave behind her customary floppy hat because the sun would be low. Instead, remembering her father's exhortation through the years, she took a few moments to apply a sunblock. No need to court skin cancer.

Only a sprinkling of people would be on the beach at this hour. The thought was reassuring. She was in no mood to socialize.

She walked down the stairs to a deserted beach. The typical pre-dinnertime scene met her gaze. A scattering of dogs, happily unleashed for a late afternoon romp, cavorted on the stretch of sand. The atmosphere of comfortable solitude was a balm to her raw nerves.

Anne settled herself near the water's edge. One by one the dogs were withdrawn, though not without some vociferous objections. Far out she spied fishing boats coming in for the day. She sat up at attention. Was that somebody in the water? The lifeguard was off-duty at this hour. The water was rough. The swimmer ought to come in closer to shore.

Suddenly the silence of the beach was shattered by a shrill outcry. Anne leapt to her feet. She strained to see the solitary swimmer, visible only a moment ago.

"Help!" A frightened childish treble drifted to shore. "Help!"

Anne unzipped her cover-up, tossed it aside, shot to the water. The coldness momentarily halted her. Then she was swimming with swift sure strokes towards the flailing arms visible above the choppy sea.

"Don't panic," she called. "I'm coming for you."

Her heart pounded from her efforts to reach the child. Her body responding to the emergency. For a moment fear brought a tightness to her throat. Where was he? Then a water-slicked head emerged. Relief surged through her.

She reached for the little boy, dodging his efforts to clutch her about the neck. Utilizing her lifesaving training, she sought a hold that would permit her to bring him in.

"It's all right," she gasped. He was hysterical with fear, making the rescue difficult. "It's all right. I'll bring you in."

The distance to shore seemed frighteningly longer than it had appeared moments ago. Her breathing was painful. Her body strained. She'd make it, she told herself. Don't try to rush.

"Take it easy—" Unexpectedly a reassuring masculine voice came to her. She had been unaware that anybody was approaching them. "I'll give you a hand."

Grateful for approaching help, she tightened her grip on the small boy. "That's good—"

"I'll take him." The other swimmer was beside them. He manipulated with skill. "You all right?"

"Fine," she gasped.

"Head on in to shore," he ordered. "The water's getting rougher by the minute. I'll bring him in with no sweat."

As Anne stumbled out of the water, shivering in the near-dusk chill, she spied a short, wiry man, his face etched with alarm, sprinting towards her.

"Jesus Christ, they ain't gonna drown, are they?"

"No. They'll be okay." Her eyes strained for sight of them. Would they be okay?

"Why ain't there no lifeguards out here?" He was belligerent in relief.

"It's off-hours," Anne explained. She crossed to pick up the terrycloth cover-up she had discarded minutes ago. "I'm sure the little boy knows better than to swim at this time of day. He must have sneaked out of his house and come down here alone."

The man who had come to her aid walked out of the water, holding the limp but conscious child in his arms.

"Mark, you okay?" the other man called out anxiously.

"Okay," his friend soothed. "Relax, Chuck."

"What about him?" Chuck focused on the little boy.

"He swallowed a lot of water, that's all." He dropped the boy on his stomach, talked encouragingly as the youngster retched up salt water. "Chuck, run up to the house and get a blanket."

Chuck darted off towards the stairs. Mark worked over the scared little boy. Anne pulled off her cover-up again and offered it as a temporary blanket.

"I was getting nervous," Anne confessed. "Suddenly the shore seemed an awful distance away."

"I handled a couple of kids like this the summers I was a camp counselor," he said. Anne smiled. She remembered similar experiences. "My name's Mark Forrest." His eyes left the exhausted little boy to rest on her. "I'm out here for the summer."

"Anne Evans. I'm here for the summer, too." Unaccountably her heart was pounding. What was the matter with her? She still hurt from Sean's death. She didn't want a replay.

"Jimmy!" A frenzied feminine voice punctured the moment between them. "Jimmy!" A slender woman in a caftan, her face etched with terror, charged down the stairs towards the prone child.

"Mommie, I'm all right," he called weakly.

"Oh, Jimmy!" She dropped to her knees beside him, comprehending the situation. "I looked around and you weren't in the house. The TV was on, but you weren't sitting there.

Jimmy, haven't I told you to stay out of the water when the lifeguards are not at their stations?"

"I know, Mommie—" His eyes were apologetic.

"He went out a little too far," Mark said. "Anne swam out to bring him in."

"Mark took over," Anne supplemented. "It was rough out there today."

Mark was embarrassed by the woman's gratitude. With relief he spied Chuck.

"Hey, Chuck, hurry up with that blanket." He took the blanket from Chuck and draped it about Jimmy's shoulders. "I'll carry him to the house."

"I can walk," Jimmy protested. He struggled to his feet. Clutching the blanket about his chilled body.

Anne stood by with a smile as Mark and the boy's mother arranged for the return of the blanket. He was renting the weathered shingle house a few houses above her own, on a lane leading away from the ocean.

"You're cold," Mark said solicitously as Anne struggled into the comfort of the terrycloth cover-up. "You'd better go home and change." But his eyes said he was reluctant to shorten this encounter.

"Come over for hamburgers and coffee in about half an hour," she invited on impulse. Her eyes moved to include Chuck. *What's the matter with me? Why did I say that? Because I don't want to be in the house alone.* "I'm at the first house to the left of the stairs, facing the beach."

"The one with all the glass?" he asked, an odd rigidity about his face.

"Yes." All at once she was self-conscious. He knew the house. What had the neighbors said about Lila? That she was the island nymphomaniac? "I'm on vacation. The house was offered to me—" That sounded strange, didn't it? To be alone in a house when people bought shares for a bedroom on alternating weekends.

"You travel in style." He laughed, but his eyes were opaque.

"Will you come over?" Why was it so important that he would?

"We'd love to come," Mark accepted for Chuck and himself. "I'll bring some beers. Okay?"

"Great."

Anne walked away with a smile, headed towards her house. *What is the matter with me? Why did I invite them for hamburgers and coffee?*

Mark Forrest wasn't a kid, Anne analyzed as she changed from sodden swimsuit to warm slacks and a sweatshirt. He was a man. A warm, attractive man. Sean had been a kid. A sweet, charming kid who made her feel less alone. They were married one week after college graduation—which meant she was not expected to join Dad and Lila in their sprawling Chappaqua house that Lila was constantly redecorating. She wasn't expected to go out to the house on Fire Island.

Anne picked up her swimsuit from the floor and carried it into the bathroom. She moved into the living room, dropped to her haunches before the fireplace. At the slightest pretense of a chilly evening she enjoyed a fire. Like Dad. He always made sure there was firewood available.

She balled up sheets of newspaper, tucked them into the grate. She chose a pair of small logs from the box beside the fireplace, interspersed some kindling. Dad had placed the necessities here in readiness for their first spring weekend out here, she thought, tears welling in her eyes.

Brushing aside the fresh grief that threatened, she reached for a match from the box atop the mantel. In moments a fire glowed in the grate. All right, go to the kitchen and prepare the hamburgers.

In minutes hamburgers were ready to go into the broiler. A bowl of salad sat waiting in the refrigerator. Mark said he would bring beer. Later they would have coffee with the éclairs defrosting down below.

The door chimes sounded almost shrill in the silence of the house. Anne hurried to the door. Mark was alone. For a moment she was wary.

"Chuck likes disco and Scotch. I sent him on a search," Mark explained casually and held up a six-pack. "Where shall I put this?"

"In the fridge." She relaxed. Mark Forrest was not looking to jump into bed with her. He was lonely. It shone from his eyes.

"I could smell the wood burning as I came up to the house. That's one of the great scents in this world." He smiled, yet seemed strangely ill at ease.

"Especially near the ocean." She, too, loved the scent of a wood-burning fireplace.

"Can I help?" He stared about the room with a disconcerting air of distaste.

"You don't like this house," she guessed. "It turns you off."

"It's sensational," he contradicted. "I'm not used to such splendor." Now his smile was wry. "It's a little different from where I've been living for the past few years."

"Where was that?"

She was aware of the split-second hesitation before he replied.

"A farm up near the Canadian border. Very rugged. Very simple." His eyes were shutting her out. *Why?* "I dropped out of college at the end of my junior year and went up there with a couple of buddies. We wanted to try living off the land." His voice was strained. "We were deep into environmental problems. You know the scene. We just came back a few days ago—"

"Where do you live now?"

Mark laughed.

"In the middle of Manhattan. Wall-to-wall pollution and forty miles from the threat of nuclear disaster."

For a moment an oppressive silence hung over them.

"Lead me to the onions," Mark ordered with calculated flipness. "You weren't planning on serving hamburgers without onions?"

"That would be sacrilegious." She picked up his mood.

In the kitchen they talked about ecology, violence in the cities, politics. Their voices grew heated with intensity. Mark Forrest and she were kindred spirits, Anne thought with pleasure.

They transferred themselves with hamburgers, salad, and beers to the floor before the fireplace. With Beethoven on the stereo, the fire sending sensuous warmth into the room, Anne talked about her job. Flattered by Mark's obvious interest. She told him about the situation involving Perez and Smith and Joey. She repeated Chris's assessment.

"Chris is right." Mark's eyes were contemptuous. "Don't lose any sleep over those little sociopaths. Somebody forgot to build a conscience into kids like those. Nothing's going to change them."

"I suppose if we threw them on a desert island and tried to reeducate them over a period of years, we might be of some help." Anne was somber. "I have hope for one of the boys."

"Don't be optimistic about those kids," Mark warned again. "The bookies would give you a thousand to one against it. And I don't mean just kids from disadvantaged backgrounds," he pinpointed. "Some very classy people move through this world without conscience. Some of them are lucky. You find them at the top of the heap in business and politics and the professions." His eyes were angry. "They don't give a damn about whom they hurt. So long as they profit." Now his eyes seemed to search deep within her soul for a pregnant moment. "What do you say we go for a walk on the beach?"

"I'd love it." Anne's face was radiant.

"You'll need a sweater," he told her. "I'll put another log on the fire while you get it. That way it'll keep going while we're away."

The beach was deserted except for a man and a woman jogging at the water's edge. The other two outdistanced Anne and Mark—strolling in comfortable silence. Moonlight cast a pale gold glow over the sand, lent glints of gold to the ocean. Stars were a glorious array of diamonds in the sky.

"Ooh—" Anne's voice deepened in awe. "Did you see that shooting star?" Her gaze clung to the sky.

"Remember when we were kids and how we'd watch for a shooting star in the night sky?" Mark reminisced. "God, that seems a million years ago—"

"There are nights that seem to last a million years—" All at once Anne was somber. "But never out here," she lied with an effort at lightness.

"I love this beautiful quiet." A tenderness crept into Mark's voice. "No raucous noises. No shrieks in the night." In the spill of moonlight she saw his face tighten as though in ugly recall. He'd left the city, she thought, and gone to the farm. But that hadn't been enough. What haunted him? "This stillness is almost like a symphony—"

"No garbage trucks at three a.m., no boom boxes screeching in the middle of the night—and no cars," Anne

47

added in triumph. "Is there any other place in this country that can claim that?"

"The great gas guzzlers," he said with contempt. "Why did we fight the Gulf War?" he challenged, "except for oil?"

"But we pulled out too soon," she said impatiently.

"We'll pay for that some day," he predicted.

They moved into a heated discussion of the American support of Iraq in earlier years, then into talk about the Democratic convention just ahead.

"My mother was deep into politics." Mark's face was tender in recall. "My father—he died six years ago—was always too busy. Mom cared about people. Still does—"

"My dad was like that, too," Anne said softly.

"I remember—when I was about ten—setting up a table on a main street in town with my older sister to hand out leaflets plugging Jimmy Carter and Walter Mondale." He chuckled. "And on a cold day Mom came trotting out with a pot of steaming hot chocolate for us." He took a deep breath. "Mom was special."

"Like my dad." Oh yes, Anne told herself again—with a feeling of having made a great discovery—she and Mark were kindred spirits.

She was startled when Mark suggested they call it a night. What had triggered that? she asked herself guiltily. *Something I said?* She searched her mind in vain.

"It's been great talking with you—" Despite his casual—almost dismissive—air, something deeper slipped through to her. "I'm glad we managed to bring that little kid in safely."

"Right." *Don't misinterpret this encounter. Mark doesn't want it to go anywhere.* "He won't be sneaking out of his house alone again."

"I'll walk you back to your place—"

"No need—" She managed a faint smile. "We don't worry about crime out here."

"I'll walk you back," he insisted, suddenly grim. "We're living in a changing world."

Fog was rolling in from the ocean as Mark walked from Anne's house. He glanced at his watch, squinting in the dim light. Relishing the scent of the sea as he moved towards his own house. Only eleven o'clock. Why the hell had he broken off a lively, good-humored discussion so suddenly? Anne had been disappointed.

The thing he'd missed most in prison was stimulating conversation. He missed the nights in the dorm—and later in the off-campus apartment he had shared with two other students—when they had talked till dawn. Driving to West Point on impulse to watch the sunrise. The late October afternoon when they'd driven out to Montauk to walk on a deserted beach and seen an incredible harvest moon.

He had wanted desperately to make love to Anne. But how could he think about making love to Anne Evans in Lila Schrieber's house? What would Anne say if she knew he was fresh out of stir, after serving six years on charges of raping Lila Schrieber?

He was making too big a deal of this thing. He had not been near anybody since the night the fuzz picked him up on the beach—he'd react this way to any good-looking woman. Yet instinctively he knew this was not true. Anne Evans was very special.

Stay away from her, he exhorted himself. Anne deserved more than a summer shack-up job. That was all there could ever be for them.

Chapter Six

Mark awoke to a dismal drizzle. Welcoming the beautiful stillness, so foreign to the waking up clamor of the past six years. The only sounds the cawing of a pair of sea gulls close by. An affirmation of his freedom.

He lingered in bed for a few moments, then with a sudden sense of urgency hurried into the bathroom to shower and dress. They weren't on vacation—they had a mission to accomplish.

He relished the luxury of his own bathroom. He'd loathed the communal showers, the lack of privacy in prison. He chuckled now—remembering Chuck's amazement that each of the two bedrooms had its own bath.

"So this is how the rich and famous live!"

His family was neither rich nor famous, but to Chuck—who grew up in South Bronx tenements—to own a house on Fire Island was the height of luxury. To live in Manhattan on the Upper West Side was luxury. All this was something unimaginable to Chuck and his buddies. They saw only two classes—the poor and the rich. They didn't recognize the great middle class.

Enough of playing the vacation scene, Mark exhorted himself. He had an operation to put into action. Late this afternoon Chuck was scheduled to go into the city to begin to line up their team. He was confident this would be no problem. "Hey, it'll be a snap. That's my territory—I know where to look."

He himself needed to go over in his mind—for the hundredth time—each step to be followed. Chuck would handle his end. Tomorrow morning he himself would tackle "Mr. Brooks"—the first on a list of prospective high-paying "clients." He'd rehearse in his mind the meeting with Brooks. It must go well.

Showered, shaved and dressed, he walked into the kitchen, was startled to see Chuck sitting at the dining table and playing solitaire. He was bored out of his skull, Mark interpreted.

"I ain't heard a sound or seen a body since I got up two hours ago," Chuck complained. "Not even a phone call. It's like livin' in solitary." Something he'd considered intolerable in prison.

"We don't have phone service," Mark pointed out. He wanted this feeling of being unreachable. He called Mom every other Sunday night—that was a ritual. "We need to make a call, they've got public phones down in the village. But why did you get up so early?" Mark opened the fridge, brought out eggs, bacon, bread. They'd have to do some food shopping, he told himself. All Chuck remembered to buy was beer. Now he walked over to the range to put up breakfast. It was obvious that Chuck had not even bothered with coffee. "You said you'd been sleeping till ten a.m. when you first got out," Mark recalled.

"It's crazy. I was used to gettin' up at five in the slammer. Then I'm outta stir and sleepin' the mornin' away. Now all of a sudden I'm goin' back to wakin' up early." Chuck seemed fascinated by the activities at the range. "You know how to cook?" Chuck seemed impressed.

"Enough so we'll eat decently." Mark reached to bring

down the coffee and percolator, conscious of the long years when such activity had been denied him. When he was in his early teens, he'd offered one weekend when they were all out here to make Sunday breakfast for the family. It had become a ritual—with Mom providing instructions from time to time. "And it won't be hamburgers or pizza three times a day."

He didn't mind the rain, Mark thought while he focused on making sure the bacon was crisp, the sunny-side eggs not overdone. A steady rainfall was oddly relaxing. Later he'd buy a bundle of firewood, search for driftwood on the beach. They'd have a fire going tonight.

Traitorously his mind focused on Anne while he pretended to listen to Chuck's raunchy recital of his pre-prison love life.

"Man, I knew how to treat the chicks in them days," Chuck bragged. "And I'm makin' up now for the time in the slammer."

He'd missed a special segment of his life, Mark analyzed with a sense of loss. The girls he had known were college kids like himself. It had been a time to experiment. College was a whole new world.

He remembered his first year at Columbia—the drinking sprees. Staggering freshmen throwing up all over the campus. The first heady taste of sex.

Most kids at Stuyvesant were too busy fighting to keep up their grades—with an eye on the SATs—to play in the sex scene. So many of them—like himself—with the long bus/subway commute to cope with, he thought with wry humor. Sure, they'd played briefly in the pot scene—but no serious drugs.

Now—all of a sudden—he was out in the world. Like an actor opening in a play but with no rehearsal time. He was twenty-six years old—not a kid anymore. No women in his life to bridge the gap between twenty and twenty-six.

Anne wasn't a kid. She was a woman. But what the hell could there ever be for Anne and him? The world wouldn't believe he was innocent of any crime. To everybody on the outside he was an ex-con. He was pushing his way into a new life that would horrify Anne Evans.

After breakfast Mark walked in the diminishing drizzle to the store where New York City newspapers were sold. When he returned with the *New York Times*, he found Chuck pacing about the living room.

"I was thinkin'. Maybe I oughta take an early ferry into the city insteada waitin' until evening." Chuck was self-conscious. "I mean, there ain't no action out here. I can get an early start on linin' up our team."

"That makes sense," Mark agreed. Chuck was bored out here—he'd find diversion in the city. He'd wait until evening to round up a prospective team. The early hours would be playtime. "You'll pick me up with the car as planned. Tomorrow morning." To drive him to their conference with Mr. Brooks. "But stay out of trouble," he warned, his eyes holding Chuck's. "We've got something great going—don't be a jerk and screw it up."

"I won't," Chuck protested with an injured air. "I'll just play a little pool, eat like it's goin' out of style—then in the evening, the way we planned, I'll start feeling out kids who look right for the job."

"Run down to the ferry," Mark told him. "Check out the ferry schedule. Your ferry this morning. My ferry tomorrow morning—when you'll pick me up at the other side." They each had a copy of the Long Island Rail Road schedule.

By eleven a.m. the rain had stopped, though the sky remained overcast. Mark walked with Chuck to the ferry.

"Stay out of trouble," Mark warned Chuck again and dug out the key to his mother's apartment. "Stay at the apartment. Set the alarm so you don't oversleep." So until he started sizing up kids, Chuck would look for a movie that showed the violent films he liked, play pool, go somewhere for a steak dinner. He knew to keep his nose clean.

Mark saw Chuck off on the ferry, headed back to the house. Despite his determination to steer clear of Anne, she dominated his thoughts. The hours with her last evening had been special.

Late in the afternoon he gave in to his feelings, went over to the Schrieber house and rang the bell. He'd never be comfortable here. Anne said she'd been "offered the house." By whom? Who owned the place now? He couldn't bring himself to ask her.

"The rain's stopped," he said when Anne came to the door. He saw the glow of candid welcome his presence evoked. "Feel like a walk along the beach?"

"Let me get a sweater." She pulled open the door to allow him to enter.

"You'll need it," he agreed.

"I'll just be a minute—"

Mark waited in the foyer while Anne went off into one of the bedrooms. It was crazy to feel so uneasy in Lila Schrieber's house. Correction—Lila Schrieber's late house. The house seemed to taunt him. His whole life had been turned around because of what was supposed to have happened here.

In a few moments Anne returned, pulling on a long, sea-blue bulky knit sweater, her bare feet now encased in sneakers.

"It looks as though the sun's trying to come out again." She smiled, but she seemed uncertain, Mark thought. Something so sweet and vulnerable about her.

"I put in a special order," he joshed, reaching for the door. Something so appealing about her. He felt a yearning to protect her. To make her feel all was right with her world.

"Would you like some coffee first?" she offered.

"Let's go to the beach." His tone was almost abrupt. He didn't want to stay here in the house alone with Anne. Not unless he could make love to her. "Coffee later—"

Under a gray sky Mark and Anne walked endlessly along the beach, deserted except for a man jogging at the water's edge, though he suspected people would be wandering out again. The rain was over.

Today Anne told him about her husband's tragic accident.

"We were kids. Sean was mad about hang gliding. He'd just persuaded me to give it a whirl. And then he was killed. We'd been married only ten months."

"That was rough," Mark sympathized.

"Then last October—when they'd come out to close up the house—my father and stepmother were killed in a smashup on the Long Island Expressway." Her eyes shone with fresh pain. "By a drunken driver hitting eighty miles an hour."

"That was rough," Mark said. He couldn't talk about his own father's death. Dad had killed himself when Mark was convicted of raping Lila Schrieber. It wasn't that Dad thought he was guilty, Mom insisted. He couldn't face his business associates with a son in prison. But Mom had stuck with him all the way. Never for a moment had Mom believed he was guilty.

"I keep waiting for something else horrible to happen," she confessed. "I'm not superstitious—but you know the old bit about bad things and good things happening in threes—"

"Only good things are in store for you," he said with conviction. *But I wouldn't be good for her.*

55

"Right," she said, her smile defiant. "I won't consider anything else." But Anne Evans had been in her own private prison these last years, Mark recognized.

Now he became aware of hunger. "What about an early seafood dinner?" Mark asked and suggested the seafood restaurant favored by his mother.

Her face lighted. "That sounds great."

They left the beach, sought out the popular restaurant. The lighting low, fresh flowers on every table. Only one table was occupied at this early hour—occupied by four women of what his mother used to call "a certain age." Their conversation was convivial yet muted.

A cordial hostess led Anne and Mark to a private corner table.

"Is this all right?" she asked. A glint in her eyes said this was a romantic evening for them.

"It's fine," Mark told her, and Anne nodded in agreement.

The hostess gave each an oversized menu. "Enjoy your dinner."

Mark stared at the open menu without seeing. His mind darting back through the years. This was where the family had celebrated his eighteenth birthday. For a little while the otherwise charming restaurant was ghost-haunted for him. He was remembering the sentiment-sloshed night when Dad gave him an overly expensive watch for his birthday while they gorged on lobster. Even Mom had been shocked.

Dad had a way of buying over-expensive gifts, as though to compensate for his absences. That was why the Fire Island house was so important to his sisters and himself. Once out here Dad belonged to the family.

Now he and Anne made a game of choosing their dinner. Seafood, of course—though for the allergic or otherwise dis-

56

inclined, there were chicken and beef selections. Their waiter arrived, pad in hand, smiled indulgently as they debated.

"All right, let's wrap this up," Anne decided. "You order the scallops in white wine and I'll have the shrimp Rockefeller and we'll share—"

"We'll both have the vichyssoise," Mark told their waiter, "and the cucumber salad, with mint and scallions."

Over a superb seafood dinner Mark and Anne talked with mutual urgency about the needs of the world. He was startled when she confided her fears about remaining in social work.

"I was so sure—back in junior high—that I wanted to spend my life in social work. I think my father was pleased— though he would have liked me to have gone to law school— like himself."

Mark froze. "My early plans—my first year at Columbia— was to go on to law school." *Her father was a lawyer—probably a friend of Lila Schrieber's husband. That's how she acquired the house for the summer. A payoff to Anne's father for help on some case?*

"What changed your mind?" she asked. "About law school," she added because he was staring into space, as though removed from the moment.

"Fate," he said with a vague gesture. "It wasn't meant to be." He forced a smile. "But why are you having last-minute doubts about social work?"

"I'm a social worker in one of Manhattan's 'bad' junior high schools. I try so hard, but there's so little I can do. Chris—the senior social worker at our school—says there's no way we can change these young sociopaths. But there are others who could be salvaged but are falling through the cracks."

"You do the best you can—" All at once he was uncomfortable. *She's talking about the kids Chuck is interviewing to-*

night. But they're like her friend Chris says—sociopaths. "Nobody can expect more."

"But it's not enough," Anne reproached with an air of defeat. "How do we cope with parents who have no sense of responsibility, who leave young kids to fend for themselves? The schools can't replace parents."

"You'll feel differently after a couple of weeks out here," he encouraged. But he felt flooded by guilt. These were the kids Chuck was bringing into their operation at this very moment. *Damn, I don't want to talk about this!* "What are we having for dessert?" He redirected the conversation. "Something obscenely rich," he decreed with an effort at lightness.

Again, they made a game of choosing dessert. Anne wavered between Black Forest cake and bread pudding with Bourbon sauce.

"What are you having?" she asked Mark.

"I was thinking about the bananas with rum." He turned to the waiter. "Will it be ignited at the table?"

"Oh yes," the waiter assured him.

"I had that once on a school trip to New Orleans." Anne's smile was dazzling. "It sounds great!"

"Let's have one order of the bananas in rum and one Black Forest cake," Mark said. *How can I be so light-headed?*

"And we'll share," they chorused together.

They lingered over their shared desserts and coffee. In a corner of his mind Mark asked himself how things were going with Chuck. Would he come up with the kids that were essential? Chuck knew these kids. He'd been one of them once. *Relax, everything's going according to schedule. Enjoy this evening.*

After dinner Anne invited him back to her place for a glass of wine and music. It seemed so natural, so right, Mark told himself while he prepared a fire in the grate. Anne had gone out to the kitchen for the wine and glasses.

There, he told himself with satisfaction—the logs were beginning to burn. In minutes they'd have a healthy blaze in the grate. He crossed to her pile of CDs, approved her choice of classical music. He slid a CD of Beethoven's *Eroica* into place, flipped the switch. Music swelled into the room. The symphony's drama, its violent transitions, fitted his mood tonight.

Anne returned with wine glasses and bottle, dropped beside him on the sofa. Sitting here before the fireplace with a glass of Chablis in one hand, he sensed that all he had to do was reach out and bring Anne into his arms. She would respond. Yet he restrained himself.

The prospect of lying in bed with Anne beside him for the rest of the night was unnerving. He'd never wanted so desperately to make love. What was the matter with him? Close to six years in stir—that was the matter with him.

But Anne was special. Like him she had been through a kind of hell. *Damn it, no. Don't get serious about Anne. What can there be for Anne and me except a few weeks at Fire Island? Lila Schrieber killed anything else for us. There's no room in Anne's life for an ex-con.*

Absurdly early he made a move to leave. He saw Anne's astonishment. Her quickly masked disappointment.

"I have to be on an early ferry in the morning," he told her. "Business in the city." Not exactly in the city—but off the island. "It may be an all-day deal. May I stop by when I come back?"

"I'm having dinner with Doris Rainey tomorrow evening. An old friend here on the island. I'll be back no later than ten. Drop by any time up till midnight. I'll be sitting up reading." Tonight Anne seemed unfamiliarly serious.

"See you tomorrow night for sure," he said. "I won't be that late."

Did Anne wonder what business took him into the city? She'd shove him out of her life this instant if she knew.

Chapter Seven

Rain beat against the windows of the tenement flat where Joey Devlin lived with his mother. A puddle formed beneath each northern window because the frames were warped and ill-fitting. Joey whistled as he worked with oil pastels on the sketchpad spread across his unmade bed.

Ever since Miss Evans gave him the pad and the pastels three months ago, he worked at a picture when he was uptight and scared. Why did Ma have to talk the way she did to Miss Evans? He'd wanted to kick her teeth out!

He didn't want to go with Luis and Frank to rip off those kids. But if he didn't, they'd think he was chicken. He paused before the sketchpad. Miss Evans said maybe someday he'd make money with pictures.

Joey stiffened at the pounding on the door. That couldn't be Ma comin' home. Her old man would kill her for quittin' this early.

"Yeah?" he called out. Wary of any intrusion.

"Joey, what the hell are you doin' sittin' at home?" Frank demanded.

"I'm busy." Frank and Luis meant trouble. Let 'em just go away.

"Come on, open up," Luis ordered. "We gotta meet a guy about a job."

Joey went into the kitchen and opened the door. *A job!* Did that judge in the Family Court scare them shitless, too? They always said reform school was a big joke.

"What kinda job?" Joey stared from Luis to Frank, suspicious about the kind of job that they could land at their ages. But the prospect of money stirred him to pleasurable anticipation. If he made some money, he'd buy a present for Miss Evans. She'd never expect him to do somethin' like that. Maybe he'd go back to that museum Miss Evans took him to twice to show him the paintings by that kook who cut off an ear and sent it to a hooker.

"José down at the pool hall says this guy's been hangin' around all evenin'. He's lookin' for a few kids our age who're quick on their feet. It's a lotta loot." Luis's eyes glistened. "He gave José a sawbuck just to make the connection. José says we gotta be at the pool hall by midnight."

"Who's gonna pay us a lotta loot?" Joey was skeptical. "Look, I don't want no more trouble."

"Hey, no trouble," Frank clucked. "We just gotta bring proof we ain't thirteen yet."

"How're we gonna do that?" Joey stalled.

"Our birth certificates, asshole." Frank pulled a piece of paper from his pocket. "You got one. Everybody's got one. My old lady keeps 'em with her welfare papers."

"We ain't on welfare," Joey said with shaky pride.

"Get your birth certificate and let's go down to the pool hall." Luis was impatient.

"I don't know where it is." Joey didn't want them to go beyond the kitchen. They'd see the sketchpad across the bed. That was somethin' between Miss Evans and him. He hid it under his bed when Ma was home. She never bothered cleanin' under the bed—she'd never see it. "I'll ask my old lady when she comes home."

Frank and Luis exchanged a glance.

"Okay," Frank decided. "We'll go down to see this guy and tell him you can prove how old you are. You just can't do it tonight."

"What kinda job is he talkin' about?" Joey was uneasy.

"We talk to the guy, we'll find out." Luis gave him a playful shove. "Don't worry. We ain't turnin' no tricks for him," he jeered. "Who wants to run around buyin' Preparation H every week?"

Chapter Eight

Chuck felt a cockiness he had not experienced for years as he played pool with a small-time hood he'd known since he was eight. At nine he was running errands for him—for a buck a throw. Nothin' like havin' money in your pocket, he thought with satisfaction.

"Hey, Chuck, you lookin' for some action?" the hood asked. "Or will your probation officer screw it up for you?"

"Man, I got action," Chuck bragged. "Big stuff." At intervals he looked over towards Tony—the druggie he'd hired to round up prospective kids. Tony was waiting for them to show. "Come on, play pool."

Earlier in the day—caught up in the drama of his situation, discarding the prospect of a high action movie—Chuck had screened out four prospects. Mark said to bring in six or seven. They'd use three for the first round, hold the others on standby for the next assignment.

It was like he had never been away from the South Bronx, Chuck thought. Everything was laid out just the way it used to be. The same tenements and fire escapes—where people slept on hot nights. The same non-air-conditioned project that shrieked of bad living. But he knew how to handle this scene. This was his turf.

"Tony, we need a few sharp kids. They gotta be under thirteen. Kids who ain't afraid of what goes down in Family

Court. They'll make so much loot their eyes'll pop out."

Tony knew enough not to ask questions. He was satisfied to take the money and pin down the kids. But he never guessed what Mark had set up. Chuck grinned. Nobody would ever guess—except their clients.

Chuck's eyes left the pool table to seek out Tony again. Okay, action now! Tony was walking in his direction. Three kids followed behind him with looks on their faces that he recognized. They were suspicious but greedy.

Tony said they'd all been in and out of Family Court. Young as they were—twelve—they'd pulled some rough stuff. They lived in Tony's building in the project. He swore they were okay.

Chuck swaggered to where Tony waited now with the three boys.

"You all under thirteen?" He was skeptical about the two hulks who looked like fourteen or fifteen. The third was slight, looking barely twelve.

"Luis and me, we got our birth certificates," the biggest one told Chuck. "I'm Frank. That's Luis." He nodded towards the short Hispanic. "Joey, he's gonna have his by tomorrow."

"You been through Family Court?" Chuck probed.

"Man, what's that gotta do with this job?" Luis was hostile.

"You wanna see ten grand?" Chuck was cool. "Maybe in three weeks."

"Ten grand to split between us?" The small, skinny kid—Joey—was about to piss in his pants with excitement, Chuck thought.

"Ten grand each," Chuck told them. "It's gonna take some trainin'. But if the boss likes you, you're in."

"What do we hafta do?" Frank exuded excitement. It didn't matter what he had to do.

"Lemme see your birth certificates." Chuck extended a hand.

Luis and Frank handed over their birth certificates. He hadn't seen a twelve-year-old as big as Frank—and with a build to match—since that creep he knew in junior high who beat up the principal and raped the girls' gym teacher.

"You two be at Tony's pad in three hours," Chuck ordered and turned to Joey. "If you got your birth certificate, you come, too. But if you ain't got it, don't show," he warned. "And don't try to bring in somebody else's birth certificate. I know your name." His eyes moved from one to the other of them. "Okay, that's it. See you in three hours." He glanced at his watch, as though making a major appointment. "If you're lucky and the boss likes you, you'll be rich."

In two hours and forty minutes Frank, Luis, and Joey were at Tony's door.

"Come inside," Chuck ordered, glorying in his new position.

"You—" he focused on Joey. "You got your birth certificate?"

"Yeah—" Eagerly Joey pulled it from a pocket of his cut-off jeans, held it out to Chuck.

"Okay," Chuck said after fast perusal of the beat-up document. "Now sit down—" He pointed to the unmade cot that served as a sofa. "And I'll tell you what you'll do to earn your ten grand."

Chapter Nine

Mark stood before the bathroom medicine chest mirror. He switched on the trio of lights above to relieve the depressing grayness of the morning. Running the electric razor over his face, he inspected his reflection with irritation. *Why do I look so tense?*

He inspected his watch when the razor had made its final trek over his chin. Plenty of time to finish dressing and walk down to the dock for the next ferry. Chuck would meet him with the car on the other side.

He unplugged the razor, pulled it apart for cleaning. Anne invaded his thoughts despite his resolution to focus on business. Sure, he was dying to sleep with her. But there was more than that between Anne and him. Nowhere in this world would he ever find someone so right for him. *But it was too late.*

He left the bathroom, went into the bedroom to dress. Brooks would appreciate his expensive business suit. The Yves St. Laurent shirt. Brooks had managed to acquire a facade of culture and polish along with his new name.

With an acute sense of destination Mark left the house. A pair of bronzed, trunk-clad young boys were dragging wagons piled high with luggage, their spirits unhampered by the overcast skies. As he strode past them, the first drops of rain began to fall.

The ferry carried a light passenger load this morning. Despite the weather Mark remained on deck. The solitary passenger thus inclined. He leaned against the railing, relishing the salt spray that brushed his face, not allowing his mind to focus on the meetings that Chuck had arranged for today.

Chuck was waiting at the ferry for him. As he touched land, he felt the spasmodic drizzle become a downpour. He sprinted towards the car. Chuck leaned forward to throw open the door for him.

"Hi ya, Attorney." This morning Chuck, too, seemed tense. Knowing they were close to picking up a quarter of a million dollars within the next few weeks was enough to make Chuck tense. All tax-free. "How do you feel?"

"Ready to do business." Mark was crisp.

Not until they were away from the ferry and headed for the palatial estate of Mr. Brooks did Chuck admit to some anxiety.

"I set up the appointment," he pointed out, "but that ain't no guarantee they're buyin'."

"Selling them is my job." Mark refused to be perturbed.

Night after night he had lain awake in his cell planning this operation. It was infallible. *Nothing* could go wrong. The courts proved this to him at regular intervals.

Mark kept his eyes on the strip of glistening road ahead. His mind raced. Instead of pleading a case before the bar, he'd plead before the ultra-rich head of a top Mafia family. His fees would compare, over the next few months, to what New York's fanciest attorneys might collect on a big case.

"We make a left here. It's a half mile down." Chuck punctured the silence that for the past five minutes had been broken only by the sound of rain pounding on the roof of the car.

They drove along a 300-foot frontage of high, stuccoed

wall, then swung in towards a pair of tall, wrought iron gates that bisected the enclosure. A stocky six-footer with bulging hip moved forward.

"Mark Forrest and Chuck Ryan," Mark told him. "Mr. Brooks is expecting us."

"Out," the man ordered, moving towards the car. They emerged to be frisked. "Okay."

They returned to the car. The guard swung one gate aside to admit them. They drove up an avenue of lush green trees that rose to impressive heights, into the circular driveway before the house.

"Mr. Brooks knows how to live." Mark inspected the dazzling replica of an Italian villa that lay to their right. Terrace upon terrace rose on either side. To their left, in the midst of a sweep of meticulously cared-for lawn, was a huge swimming pool, deserted this morning.

"Be cool, Attorney," Chuck exhorted with a taut grin.

"An Academy Award performance," Mark promised. "Come on before they send a search party for us."

They left the car, walked to the entrance. Mr. Brooks, as he was known to his neighbors, was into hard drugs, prostitution, and the numbers racket on a massive scale. But he had been sufficiently intrigued by what they had to offer to set up this appointment, Mark reminded himself.

A woman in a maid's uniform opened the door and ushered them into the domed foyer.

"Mr. Brooks is expecting us," Mark said. But she knew, of course.

"This way." She led them along the marble-floored entrance corridor, its walls salmon pink, flanked with Oriental statues that were meant to indicate that Mr. Brooks was a man of expensive tastes. "In here." She opened a pair of heavy oak doors.

Behind a huge executive desk, beyond an expanse of Oriental rug, sat a small, keen-eyed, luxuriously tailored man with a silver-tinged beard and moustache and a Caribbean tan. On a wood-paneled wall behind him hung an impressively mounted swordfish. Mark doubted that Mr. Brooks had caught it.

Brooks was not the cinematic conception of "the Don," Mark thought as he advanced into the oversized room with a calculated air of deference, Chuck at his heels. As he approached, Mark evaluated the pair of burly hoods who flanked Brooks. Muscles, despite the window dressing.

"I will allow you ten minutes, Mr. Forrest." Brooks was brusque. His voice refuted the veneer of polish. He issued no invitation to his visitors to sit. "Only because a friend asked me to do this." His eyes dismissed Chuck as a menial.

"We have a valuable service to offer, Mr. Brooks," Mark said in the low-keyed fashion he sensed would reach the other man. He had rehearsed this endless times. *Don't muff it.* "There are certain jobs you wish done without repercussions. We can guarantee this."

"How can you guarantee?" Brooks demanded. His eyes were cynical. "You have the whole police department in your pocket?"

"We have better. We have the law on our side. The way a job is handled now, a blood bath follows. That's bad for you. We assure this can't happen with us. Each hit will appear a senseless act of violence. The kind we read about in the tabloids every day. The murderer will be apprehended and serve his term—"

"Mr. Forrest, what kind of fairy tale are you handing me?" Brooks was impatient. The two hoods moved forward. Mark knew Chuck and he were seconds from being evicted. "What murderer serves his term without talking?"

"A twelve-year-old sociopath, Mr. Brooks," Mark said, "who will be paroled from reform school in three months. With bad luck he might have to serve twelve to eighteen months—but with the overcrowding today that's unlikely. He'll be paid ten thousand of the two hundred fifty thousand per hit you pay my organization." He allowed himself a cynical smile. "To these twelve-year-olds, that's a fortune."

"The guy's crazy!" the taller of the hoods bellowed. "I'll throw him out."

"Wait, Vito," Mr. Brooks intervened. "I want to hear more of this fairy tale."

"I have here in my pocket," Mark advanced into a harder sell, "material to back up what I'm saying." He pulled out the collection of newspaper and magazine clippings prepared for this moment. Spread them before Brooks. Brooks frowned, picked up a pair of glasses and slid them into place as he reached for a *New York Times Magazine* article: "I Can Kill Because I'm 14."

"You don't read the newspapers regularly," Brooks reprimanded. "They passed a law. A fourteen-year-old can be tried for murder now."

"But it doesn't happen," Mark shot back. "Not in any major city. Read these—" He pinpointed items on the desk. "Where can the courts send a fourteen-year-old convicted of murder? They drop the charge to manslaughter. The kid is switched to Family Court for sentencing. It's eighteen months tops, and he's out on parole. And in the case of my boys—all only twelve," he emphasized, "they're ten thousand dollars richer. Tax-free. Read on, Mr. Brooks. Every fourteen-year-old on the street knows he can kill and get away with it. And for extra protection I use nobody over twelve."

"A fairy tale," Brooks reiterated, but with less conviction.

"Fact," Mark insisted. "We're setting up a syndicate of very young 'hit kids.' They'll accept the blame. The case is sealed because of their ages. No senseless blood baths between opposing families. A crazy kid flipped his lid and went berserk with a rod. An 'innocent bystander' was killed."

"Mr. Forrest, this sounds like a bad television show," Brooks drawled, but his eyes revealed his interest. "Where do you find your candidates?"

"I served time in stir. On a frame. I spent those years in research so that when I came out I could collect—legally—what the courts took from me. I spent five and a half years studying law books, taking sociology courses by mail. Reading newspapers and magazines. I know exactly what kids to hire. We've screened dozens of them. We have the first three on call. To guarantee you hits that will cause hardly a ripple in the news media and police circles. We can move into action in two weeks."

"You're an expensive service," Brooks said. "You're being undercut."

"Mr. Brooks, when you buy a suit, you go to the finest tailor in the country. You pay high. Because you want the best. We're the best. Nobody offers the fringe benefits we provide. A job done and no useless slaughter afterwards."

"You're forgetting something important," Brooks said with deceptive softness, and Mark tensed. "What about our message? We arrange for somebody to be eliminated, we've got a message to get across."

"Mr. Brooks, your message will get across," Mark promised. "But the receivers will be psychologically afraid to voice their suspicions. A twelve-year-old kid in a hit operation? Who would believe it?"

Brooks's face tightened.

"Five weeks ago my nephew was killed, Mr. Forrest." Mark recalled the headlines about the gangland-style murder. "A fine boy. My wife and I grieve for him. And you tell me a twelve-year-old boy can make up for that?"

"A twelve-year-old boy can, with our training, execute your target. That's what you want." Mark paused. "Wouldn't it be better to end it there before more men get killed?"

"I'm not a philosopher." Brooks squinted into space. The two hoods shuffled restlessly. "Maybe you're right, Mr. Forrest."

"We have one stipulation," Mark said. "We won't accept an assignment on anybody working outside your own field of operations. You understand me, sir?" Mark was conscious of Chuck's gasp of astonishment. Chuck had not been briefed on this angle.

Unexpectedly Brooks chuckled. "Do I detect a flavor of Robin Hood here?" But there was a glint of respect in Brooks's eyes.

"It's our one stipulation. A precaution," Mark amplified. "If innocent people get hurt, the pigs and the media yell loud and hunt hard."

"They won't have to hunt," Brooks retaliated. "Your boy lets himself get caught. Isn't that what you're saying?"

"If innocent people are involved, some smart-assed reporter might start to dig. That could endanger my future activities." Mark was cool and deliberate. "We'll check out each assignment. Once we accept, the job will be carried out. The murderer will be apprehended, tried, convicted, and serve his term. No repercussions."

Brooks leaned back in his chair, narrowed his eyes.

"You talk about repercussions, Forrest. You take on an assignment, we expect the job to be done. Fail, and you'll suffer repercussions," he warned.

"We won't fail," Mark promised. His throat was suddenly tight with the smell of success.

"Sit down," Brooks ordered. "Let's talk."

Chapter Ten

Mark leaned back in the car with a smile of subdued triumph. He had gone into the enemy camp and emerged the victor. Brooks had no idea how he was sweating it.

Neither Mark nor Chuck spoke until they drove past the gates and onto the public road.

"Attorney, you did it!" Chuck chortled with disbelief. "I was so scared I nearly pissed in my pants. But you handled it like stealin' a pencil off a blind man." He eyed Mark curiously for an instant. "What was that Robin Hood crap you threw at Brooks?"

"An inspiration of the moment," Mark lied. "To work up some respect for us."

"You coulda blown the whole deal." Chuck flinched. "No," he corrected himself. "You were smart, Attorney."

The man Brooks had fingered was unknown to him. An imperceptible nod from Chuck had reassured him that Tony Maglione was an underworld figure. The deal was sealed. Brooks would brief them on Maglione's return to the city.

"Okay, Chuck, let's get over to your pal's pad. I want to see these kids you've lined up."

"We got plenty of time to stop and eat." Chuck was reproachful. "Man, have I worked up an appetite!" He hunched over the wheel, his eyes bright with anticipation.

"He didn't even try to cut ya down on the payoff. He liked your style, Attorney."

They stopped at an expensive restaurant catering to business luncheons and suburban matrons on a spree. The lighting was soft. Pristine tablecloths, fresh flowers on every table. Chuck was self-conscious, ill at ease as he walked beside Mark into the elegantly appointed room and they were shown to a table.

"Jesus Christ, look at the prices!" Chuck whispered to Mark when they were settled over the menus.

"We don't have to worry," Mark brushed this aside. "We're in business."

Four hits—that was all they needed to pile up a million dollars. In major cities with plenty of distance between them. By the time the cops caught on to a pattern, they'd be on to fresh fields. Train one team, pull off the job, collect. Then on to the next. And what was morally wrong with this operation? They were ridding the earth of scum. Brooks read him loud and clear. Their targets would be only underworld figures. Creeps that the world would not miss.

They ate a lavish lunch, which Chuck had allowed Mark to order. Chuck struggled not to be intimidated by his unfamiliar surroundings. But even while he was uncomfortable, he glowed with an awareness of elevation in status.

Walking out of the restaurant fifty minutes later, Mark's attention was drawn to a girl at a table near the door. In profile she resembled Anne. The girl turned her head, and the illusion was destroyed. Mark frowned. Why the hell was he thinking about Anne? They belonged to different worlds. No bridge between them.

Mark and Chuck drove through the steady downpour with the radio blaring the top records of the week. Mark was silent. Replaying in his mind those final minutes with Brooks when they cemented their deal.

Before the meeting this morning everything had been con-
jecture. Now he was in business. *On Brooks's side of the fence.*
Part of him recoiled from this. But what chance had he in the
other world? An ex-con had no rights.

They cut off the Long Island Expressway and onto the
Triboro Bridge. Mark became aware of the depressing land-
scape. He frowned, ordered himself to concentrate on the
task ahead. The South Bronx was unfamiliar to him except
for shots that made their way into the TV news. But as they
arrived in the area, he had a sense of having been here before.
Chuck had been eloquent in his descriptions of his turf.

The streets were garbage-laden, the tenements run-down.
Here and there boarded-up windows told of abandoned
buildings. The rain had settled down to a muggy drizzle.
Steam appeared to rise from the asphalt. Scantily clad youngsters cavorted in the wetness, sloshing with approval in pud-
dles that appeared at every crack in the pavement.

"Nobody's gonna steal our hubcaps or take out the battery," Chuck boasted, pulling into a wedge of parking space
at the curb. He grinned at a ten-year-old who stopped a game
of catch to inspect the car. "Hey, Dino, buy yourself an ice,
then watch my wheels while you eat it." He tossed six quar-
ters, one at a time. Dino caught them, grinned, and sprinted
across to an Italian ices cart taking refuge from the drizzle beneath an awning.

"Where does this Tony live?" Mark asked, fighting impatience.

"Right around the corner," Chuck soothed and prodded
Mark in that direction.

Chuck led him into the putrid entrance to a tenement that
Mark suspected dated back to the turn of the century. They
began to climb a flight of weather-beaten, chipped stairs that
blended aromas of pot with cat, urine, and garlic.

"Tony's pad is just another two flights up," Chuck said, puffing midway up the first.

"I'm in trim," Mark said wryly. "The stairs don't bother me."

At the fourth-floor landing Chuck led the way to a door at the rear of the hall, knocked in what was obviously a signal.

A slight, ugly man of indeterminate age opened the door. A junkie, Mark sized him up.

"I got 'em here. Jesus, you keep me tied up all day," Tony complained while he covertly inspected Mark.

"Here's something for your trouble." Mark reached into his wallet for two twenties. "Blow."

"Yeah, sure." Tony's eyes were eager. He was on his way to a forty-dollar fix.

Mark closed the door behind him. The entrance to the apartment was the kitchen. He tried to conceal his distaste for the dirty, roach-infested room. Chuck swaggered into the room beyond. Mark followed.

On the unmade pair of cots, using a jumble of filthy sheets and comforters as backrests, seven twelve-year-olds lounged in self-conscious positions. The faces were different. The eyes were the same. Over-bold, suspicious, defiant. The kind of eyes Mark had seen in prison. Eyes belonging to those who used the prisons as a second home. God, he loathed punks like these! But they were his capital investment.

"Hi, kids," Chuck said with an air of high spirits. "This is Mr. Forrest." He introduced them with an air of deference meant to impress.

"I'll talk to you one at a time." Mark was brisk. "In the kitchen." A quick exit for rejects. If he found somebody workable, he'd send him to the cell-size bedroom for full briefing. "You first." He motioned to a skinny Hispanic youth wearing a gang jacket.

The first three were not for him. Mark realized this in less than a minute of conversation. Even at their tender age they were into hard drugs. He dismissed them with a twenty-dollar bill for their trouble. The next one had all the markings of a sociopath. The kind of creep that Anne would worry about, Mark thought. Her friend Chris knew better.

"Okay, we'll talk some more later, Frank." He remembered this one's name. "Go into the bedroom and wait."

The next prospect was a tall black kid already sprouting a beard. He tried to convince Mark there was a mistake on his birth certificate. He was going on thirteen, not fourteen. "Hey, man, I'm goin' on thirteen—fourteen. My old lady—she ain't so bright. Lazy, ya know. She jus' never got around to havin' my birth certificate fixed," he said nonchalantly.

Mark dismissed him with another twenty-dollar bill and continued the interviewing. The next boy, a Hispanic named Luis, was a friend of Frank. They'd been through Family Court on the same charges, Chuck had whispered to him. Luis looked at him with eyes that told Mark here was a prime candidate.

"That other kid out there? A friend of yours?"

"Joey? Oh, sure." Luis grinned. "Don't pay no attention to that baby face. Joey's okay."

Joey, too, had his birth certificate. For a moment Mark was tempted to send Joey on his way. But the three boys—one black, one Hispanic, one white and all living in the same tenement—were a team. That could work out well. Forget Joey's baby face. That wouldn't stop him from doing what the other two had done.

Mark sat down with the three chosen, explained the operation in blunt words they could understand. Not one of the three displayed any compunction about what would be required of them, he noted. But now suspicion intruded.

"Man, what makes us know you're gonna lay on that ten grand?" Frank demanded. "What proof we got you ain't gonna play us for suckers?"

Mark was prepared for this. Still, he had to struggle to conceal his distaste. "This is the way it'll go down," he said in casual tones. "I arrange for the rental of three safe deposit boxes in three different banks," Mark explained. "In each case my twelve-year-old nephew or foster child—one of you—has access to the box."

"What do ya mean, we got access?" Luis demanded, exchanging a loaded glance with Frank.

"You sign a signature card from the bank—that makes it legal for you to go into the bank and ask for the box. Then—"

"Wait up," Frank broke in. "What's this crap about a signature card?"

"Once you're in training and working out, I'll go to the bank and ask for the cards. You sign them—I take them back. That means the bank must give you access to the box whenever you come in. The day after the job is pulled, ten thousand in fifties and hundreds goes into that box. My key goes to you. Nobody else except the bank has a key. When you come out of reform school—if you get stuck with that—you go to the bank, show your birth certificate or some other ID. The clerk at the safe deposit box section will bring the box to you. You take out the cash—in fifty and one hundred bills— and blow."

"How do we know you won't go to the bank first?" Luis's dark eyes were insolent. "How do we know you'll even put the money in the box?"

"Listen to me, you son of a bitch," Mark said with cold intensity. "This is a million-dollar operation. I don't *need* your shitty ten grand. I'll blow that in one week at Vegas."

For ten minutes Mark allowed the boys to shoot questions

at him. But he knew they were in. Greed glittered from their eyes. They agreed to take it as Mark laid it out for them.

"Chuck will train you. On the actual job two of you will work. One for a hundred-dollar tip," he said and watched the hostile reproach well in the three pairs of eyes glued to him. "The other walks off with ten grand."

"Hey, you sayin' we can bust our chops with what you call trainin'—and wind up with a hundred bucks?"

"That's more greenery than you've ever held in your hands in your lifetime," Mark shot back. "But each of you will get a shot at the jackpot." *With luck on our side.* "But first you have to train," he emphasized.

"Like what?" Luis challenged and Frank nodded. Only Joey seemed too intimidated to ask questions.

"You have to learn to shoot so there's no chance of a miss. Then you have to learn the playacting part." Their eyes brightened. They were visualizing themselves as Charles Bronson or Clint Eastwood in some old movies they'd seen on TV. "You stage a fight between the two of you at the exact time we set up. At just the right moment the one who's doing the hit pulls out a piece. The other reaches for his arm. It has to look as though the shot went wild. You'll go over the mechanics of this a hundred times. Maybe more. You've got to be smooth. No slip-ups. The hit man cuts right out. The other lingers long enough to get caught. He gives the cops a lead on where the guy with the gun hangs out. A neighborhood poolroom. Whatever." Mark shrugged. "Chuck will set that up with you. But keep this in mind. When the fuzz moves in, you say you have no lawyer. The public defender will plead your case. You'll go to reform school for a few weeks or months at the most. You'll come out and pick up ten grand."

The boys left the flat. Swaggering with fresh assurance.

Pleased that he had promised them ten dollars a day "expense money" while they were in training, Mark surmised.

"I'll drive you back to Bay Shore," Chuck told Mark. "Can't have the attorney ridin' on public transportation. You gotta travel in style." Chuck loved being behind the wheel of a car. Even an eight-year-old, badly treated Plymouth. The extra driving was no hardship. "Don't I make a sensational chauffeur?"

On the long drive back to Bay Shore the rain gave way to a late afternoon sky pink with promise. Again Mark found his mind invaded by Anne Evans. He checked his watch. Added ferry travel time to the drive to Bay Shore. He'd be home early. He was impatient for Anne to be done with her socializing.

Sitting beside Chuck in the car, he pretended to be asleep.

He ached to be walking along the beach again with Anne at his side. He wanted Anne to be in his life forever. He didn't need months to realize that.

God, how ironic that she was staying in Lila Schrieber's house! Except for Lila Schrieber, today would not have happened. But what happened today, in that impressive villa near Bay Shore and the roach- and rat-infested flat in the South Bronx, put an insurmountable wall forever between Anne and him. How shitty, to find her and know she was beyond his reach.

Chapter Eleven

Anne sat on the floor with her back resting against the sofa and gazed at the smoldering logs in the grate.

"I know it's not that chilly," Doris said earlier when she'd coaxed the logs into burning, "but there's something so mellow and relaxing about a fireplace." And the scent of burning birch was wonderful, Anne thought in a rare moment of relaxation.

Doris had gone out to the kitchen to make fresh espresso for them. Tonight for the first time, Anne mused, she saw Doris as someone other than the glamorous theater person she had always appeared. But so many people had two faces. *From what is Mark hiding? He's running from something.*

Tonight Doris had talked about her three failed marriages. About her daughter seeking peace in a nomadic life with her current love along the coast of California. She told Anne about her son, now twenty-three, who suffered from severe Down's Syndrome. His expensive care sapped much of her finances.

Anne glanced up with a smile as Doris returned to the living room with a fresh pot of espresso in tow.

"Drink up, baby," Doris drawled good-humoredly as she poured. "Nobody outside of Italy makes better espresso than me." She fought back a yawn.

"You're tired," Anne said sympathetically.

"Not really," Doris refuted. "It's all that salt air." She paused. "I should be working this summer," she said with candor. "I don't know why the hell my son of a bitch of an agent messed up booking me into a package." Her eyes were uneasy. "Do you know, Annie, I haven't worked once in the past two years. That's frightening. How long can I exist on residuals? Jobs always come in cycles. Either you can't find enough time to handle all the job offers—or there's nothing." She frowned, then forced a smile. "God, I sound morbid." She scrutinized Anne. "A new man in your life these days?"

"No time," Anne dismissed this.

"Nonsense," Doris scoffed. "It's not healthy not to have a man in your life at your age." She laughed. "At any age. Without sex you grow old before your time. Not that either you or I are apt to suffer such a fate. You're really gorgeous, darling, in that understated fashion. And probably as passionate as hell."

Disconcerted, Anne focused on her espresso. She didn't want to talk about her sex life. She wasn't the type, like some of the single caseworkers she knew, to go regularly to a bar to be picked up for a night of uninvolved lovemaking. She'd have to love the man before she went to bed with him. Claire said it was enough for her just to like the guy. Over lunch last week Claire took inventory.

"I figured it out. It's been two years since I got my master's and came to New York. I've balled exactly one dozen guys in that time. But I liked them all a little."

"I'll finish my coffee and cut out." Anne faked a yawn. "The salt air's getting to me, too."

She couldn't play Claire's scene. Yet she knew Mark could sleep with her any time he chose. Was she in love with him? Could it happen that fast? Doris was right. She was passionate. Sean proved that to her.

Anne set down her cup, unwound herself and rose to her feet.

"I'll see you tomorrow. We'll both hit the sack early tonight." *She* wouldn't. She'd drape herself across the living room sofa and read. And wait for the sound of the door chimes that said Mark had returned to the island.

It was absurd the way she hated being alone in the house, she scolded herself as she opened the door and walked inside. Too many ghosts. At intervals she'd asked herself if she'd done the right thing in not telling Dad what she knew about Lila. Had he ever suspected Lila of being less than a perfect wife?

She remembered how upset he'd been when Lila was raped—right here in this house. She'd been in the Canary Islands with a group from college because she couldn't bear spending a summer at the Fire Island house with Lila.

She'd thought she would lie on the sofa and read, she derided herself later. Instead her mind traitorously digressed to Joey, moved on to Luis Perez and Frank Smith. So many screwed-up kids in the world! And Mark was right—they didn't all come from slums. They came from expensive houses in Westport and luxury co-ops on the Upper East Side. They were in high-priced private schools and ultra-rich boarding schools.

Chris kept battling with her to make her recognize the difference between screwed-up kids whom they could help and the sociopaths. Chris insisted that with Luis and Frank it was more than their feeling neglected and calling attention to themselves. Luis and Frank didn't know the difference between right and wrong. They were classic sociopaths.

"Good Lord, Anne, those two bastards are capable of murder!"

At least Chris had not included Joey in that denunciation.

What were they to do with these kids? She didn't know enough yet to cope, she thought with exasperation. With twenty years of experience Chris couldn't cope with some of their kids. But they could reach some. Like Joey. If she could be sure she was making some progress with Joey, then she'd feel she belonged in social work.

Restless, Anne left the sofa and went into the kitchen to put up a percolator of coffee. She drank too much coffee. But at least she wasn't a candidate for AA. She wasn't a chain-smoker flirting with lung cancer twenty or thirty years from now.

She put up the coffee, returned to the living room, aware of a growing chill in the air. The excuse she needed to start a fire in the grate. She crouched before the fireplace, feeding paper and kindling between the small logs. Glancing occasionally at the sunburst electric clock on one wall.

She went into the kitchen to put up the percolator. It unnerved her to realize how eager she was to see Mark. She wasn't ready to become emotionally involved again. She was tired. Overwrought from all the happenings at the office. She was too susceptible. That was all it was.

She started at the sound of the door chimes, hurried to the door. She swung it wide. Mark stood there smiling at her. In beat-up jeans, a cotton turtleneck, and windbreaker. But his eyes were in conflict with his smile. Somber, defensive, unhappy.

"Hi," she said breathlessly. "Come on in."

"I stopped at the house to change into comfortable clothes." He strode into the living room, headed for the fireplace as he pulled off his windbreaker. "That's why I'm this late."

"Was it hot in the city?" *Mark is disturbed about something. What was the business that took him into the city?* "I thought it would be."

"Wet and humid," he confirmed, dropping to the floor before the fireplace.

"I stayed around the house and read most of the day." She pointed to a batch of paperbacks spilled about one end of the sofa. *Why did Mark go into the city? Is he job hunting?* She knew so little about him. "It's great to know that I don't have to go into the office until September."

"You didn't leave the office altogether behind," he jibed. His eyes focused on the stack of books at one end of the mantel. All of them dealt with disturbed adolescents.

"I can't," she confessed. "I'm too committed. Chris says that's wrong."

"You'll change. You'll get over being a bleeding heart."

"You're angry," Anne accused. "And bitter."

"Isn't everybody?" he evaded. "The very rich are bored out of their skulls. The middle class is squeezed on every side. The poor complain because they haven't got the affluent life they see on television at least six hours every day."

"I think it's good to be angry." Anne was groping for words. "If it's used in a positive fashion." Abruptly she rose to her feet. "I'll go check on the coffee."

Anne made a point of dallying in the kitchen to put distance between Mark and herself. *I want Mark to make love to me.* This was too fast. She wasn't like Claire.

She left the kitchen and walked back into the living room. Mark was on his feet. Without a word he crossed to draw her into his arms. She made no move to withdraw. Experimentally he kissed her. Then he kissed her with hunger. It didn't matter that it was so little time that she'd known Mark. She knew she was in love with him.

Mark's mouth released hers. His eyes asked questions.

"The coffee—" Her voice was uneven.

"I'll turn it off."

She walked into the darkened bedroom, crossed to the wide window that faced the sea. It seemed such a long time ago that she had lain in Sean's arms. Sean and she had been two kids. Mark was a man. She was a woman now.

"Anne—" She heard a strange insecurity in Mark's voice. It was as though he was fearful of rejection even now.

She spun away from the window. The moonlight swathed her in eerie radiance.

"It's been a long time for me," she said with candor, moving towards him. Her voice deepened as he pulled her to him. "Oh, Mark—"

Chapter Twelve

Mark lay back on the bed—nude beneath the light blanket. He reached to turn on the lamp on the night table. A ribbon of light showed beneath the adjoining bathroom door.

It had never been like this for him before, he thought. Disturbed. It had not been the way he had imagined in those long celibate nights in his cell when he wove passionate fantasies of the first time he slept with a woman again.

He was conscious of a new dimension in sleeping with Anne. It had never been a shared experience before. Just two kids groping for a moment of excitement. Tonight it had been important to give pleasure as well as to receive it.

He was in love with Anne. Damn, he had no room in his life for a woman like Anne. He knew the kind of woman who belonged in his life.

He started at the sound of the timer in the kitchen. Anne had put up the coffee again before she went in to shower.

"I'll get it—" Anne pushed open the bathroom door. "Stay there."

He watched her stride across the bedroom. She seemed younger than she was in the floor-length blue robe that hugged her slender body. She was in love with him. She glowed with the discovery.

All he had counted on was for a summer shack-up deal. He

had to break up this scene. But he knew he would go on seeing her as long as he could.

In a gesture of impatience, he thrust aside the covers, reached for the jumble of clothes on the floor, dressed. Now he sprawled again upon the bed. In a few minutes Anne returned to the room with two mugs in tow. Her eyes widened at the sight of him fully clothed. She had expected him to stay the night.

"Coffee smells great." He leaned forward to take a mug from her. Despite his intentions to play it cool, his eyes held hers. "You're great."

"We're great," she laughed and lowered her eyes to her mug in sudden, endearing shyness. "You take your coffee black, right? No sugar—"

"Right." He shifted over on the bed so that she could sit beside him. All at once he was uncomfortable here in this room with Anne. He remembered the lies he had fed her that first night. She had believed him. She thought he was somebody special. What would she say if she knew about the kids who were going to work for him? The kinds of kids she would break her heart over if she didn't learn to be tough like that supervisor of hers. "I have to go into Bay Shore tomorrow." That was to alibi his not staying overnight. "I'll leave early."

"If you get back early enough," she said with an air of spontaneity, "come over for dinner."

"I'll make it," he promised. His eyes strayed to a framed snapshot on the night table. "Is that you?" He moved forward to pick it up.

"When I was seven. That's Dad with me. He asked a fellow tourist to take that snap of us before the Tower of London." Anne gazed with poignant wistfulness at the photograph. "Dad died last October. He bought this house the summer I was seven. I keep expecting him to come charging up the path yelling 'Annie, I'm here,' the way he did when I was little."

"You've had tough breaks."

"Scratch anybody, and you come down to blood pretty fast." She took the photograph from him and returned it to the night table.

Mark frowned, searching his mind. Where had he seen Anne's father before? He could swear he had met him.

"I'm a bleeding heart like you," Mark admitted with a wry grin. He had been a bleeding heart. "I'd planned on going to law school before I cut out for the farm." He hated lying to her. "I meant to use the degree to work for a better society. Fight within the system for changes." Bitterness crept into his voice without his awareness. "But that kind of idealism belonged to the 'sixties."

"It belongs to any period!" Anne shot back. "You've left the farm. You've come back to New York. That shows you believe there's something here for you."

"Annie, your logic's crazy," he reproached with a touch of humor. The only thing left for him was on the opposite side of the law. Annie would be sick with shock if she knew the truth about him. "I'd better cut out in a few minutes," he said abruptly. "I want to make the early ferry."

Anne walked with him to the door. Not trying to persuade him to stay over. She wondered why he was going in to Bay Shore. She couldn't figure him out.

"The fog's rolling in," he said as they lingered at the door. "It'll be as foggy as hell in the morning." But he loved seeing the island engulfed in fog.

"Seafood for dinner?" she asked when he had kissed her good night.

"Anything except whale steak. Good night, Annie."

He left the house. He intended to go home. Midway he reversed his steps and headed for the beach. It was a beautiful reassurance of his freedom that he could make this decision.

Why did the photograph beside Annie's bed keep shoving itself into his memory? Where had he seen her father before?

Mark walked slowly along the fog-shrouded beach. Fresh tension gripped him. Tomorrow morning Chuck, with the three kids, would pick him up at the other side of the ferry. They would drive out to the deserted garbage dump about which Chuck had learned in his groundwork. He would see the three punks in action. He had to be sure about them.

A cat meowed close by, then brushed up against his ankles as he paused at the water's edge. He reached down to pick up the small bundle of fur, caressed the tiny head. Where the hell had he seen Anne's father before? The question haunted him.

When Anne and he first met, Mark recalled again with rising curiosity, she'd said the house was offered to her for her vacation. Tonight she said her father bought the house the summer she was seven. All at once Mark was ice cold. *The Schrieber house.*

He remembered where he had seen Anne's father. He had seen him many times. In court. A distinguished, prematurely gray-haired man who sat beside Lila Schrieber throughout the trial. A member of the law firm of Carstairs, Schrieber, and Miller.

Anne Evans had been Anne Schrieber. She was Lila Schrieber's stepdaughter.

Chapter Thirteen

Mark stood at the railing on the ferry as the island disappeared from view. Visualizing Anne's face as he reached to kiss her good night. It had shaken him up to realize that Anne was Lila Schrieber's stepdaughter. *What strange fate was manipulating their lives?*

Anne would have chucked him out of the house if she knew who he was. But how could she know? He was Mark Forrest now. He looked little like those blurred newspaper photographs of all those years ago.

How the hell had it happened? Anne and he both coming out to the island this summer. Meeting this way. She said she'd spent almost no time at all out here since early high school. He'd sworn never to set foot out here again.

Mark smothered a yawn. He had slept little last night. He kept remembering how it had been in bed with Anne. Knowing she had wanted him to stay. He'd wanted to stay. So badly he'd wanted to stay.

Anne would have fit perfectly into that other life. The pre-stir world where he was on the road to a law degree. He had to break this up fast before she got hurt. He owed her that.

He frowned, ordered himself to concentrate on the day ahead of him. Chuck would be at the ferry with the punks for the drive to the dump. That would be their training ground.

He rehearsed in his mind every minute detail that he must

drill into those kids' heads. Chuck could take it from there. Daily workouts till their target was in town. *Stop thinking about Anne. This is what is real.*

As the ferry drew close to shore, Mark spied the green Plymouth. Chuck was right on schedule. He wouldn't let anything spoil their operation. He couldn't wait to see their first haul.

Chuck threw the car door open as he approached the passenger side.

"Betcha didn't think we'd be here on time," Chuck jeered in high good humor while the three boys on the back seat offered sleepy-eyed greetings. They'd be out of the city for hours every day, but nobody would notice, Mark guessed.

"Any kid who made you late would have been replaced," Mark said calmly. He turned around to face the kids on the back seat. His eyes moved from one boy to the other. Let them realize he would tolerate nothing short of absolute obedience.

"I bought the cooler like you said. It's loaded with soda and cold cuts," Chuck told Mark. "So none of you guys gets scared you're gonna starve," Chuck tossed exuberantly over one shoulder. He reached for the ignition. "We'll be out at the dump in twelve to fifteen minutes."

Instead of a training course for murder, this might be a picnic, Mark told himself with sardonic humor. He fought against the revulsion that welled in him. These kids were scum. Chuck was an older version of them. Left on the street Chuck would rob, sell hard drugs, even murder.

The three on the back seat were conspicuously quiet as they drove towards their destination.

"I'll call Brooks tomorrow morning, like you two set up," Chuck reminded Mark. "If he's got the snaps of the Maglione character, I'll stop by to pick them up. How long do you think it'll be before Maglione hits town?" An undercurrent of excitement laced his voice.

"You heard Brooks. Anywhere from five to ten days. Maybe earlier. We've got to be ready." A sharp edge to his voice. Those kids had to learn to be crack shots in five to ten days. Was he expecting too much of them? They'd be practicing every day for hours on end. But would it take crack shots to hit their target at close range? Be realistic, he ordered himself. These kids could handle it.

"We'll be ready, Attorney," Chuck soothed. "Everything's gonna go just right."

Chuck turned off onto a side road. "Nobody comes out here except kids who wanna practice shootin'." Chuck winked. "That's us, Attorney."

"Chuck, slow down." Annoyance laced his voice. How many times must he tell Chuck this? "We don't need to pick up speeding tickets. We'll get there soon enough." Two ex-cons reporting to probation officers couldn't afford speeding tickets.

Chuck slowed down. Nothing but silence from the three on the rear seat. Chuck had taken the car into a garage, Mark guessed. The air-conditioner was in better shape today. It would be hot as hell where they planned to practice shooting, he surmised. He'd tell Chuck to pick up shorts for the kids. No air-conditioning on their firing range.

In twenty minutes Chuck was pulling into a flat deserted area, humped at one end in a mound of miniature hills that covered garbage from earlier days. With an air of excitement the three twelve-year-olds emerged from the car. Chuck went to the trunk, opened it, brought out three street-bought guns.

"The serial numbers are filed off?" Mark asked Chuck and noted the boys' instant response to this. They felt as though they were part of some TV series, he guessed. Like "Law & Order," that cop show that fascinated Chuck.

"Come on," Chuck scoffed. "You think I don't know to do that?" He turned to the boys. "Okay, kids. Come get your pieces."

Mark noted the air of bravado they exuded. With a gun in hand, each thought he was king of the roost. Only Joey seemed a little awed.

"Remember," Mark said with the coldness he knew would earn their respect, "only one of you will have a gun when you're on a hit. But each of you gets a job. Now go out there with Chuck, and let's see you learn how to handle your piece."

Chuck had put in a lot of time on rifle ranges. He was proud of his skill. Proud that he was in charge at this point. Mark sat in the car and watched him put the three through their paces. It was a heady game at this point to the kids—but it would be death for Tony Maglione when the word came through that he was back in town.

"Man, when we gonna eat?" Frank asked when they had put in a solid two hours of target practice. "I ain't been so hungry since our welfare check got hung up for two weeks."

"Chow," Mark said, getting out of the car and heading for the trunk.

He brought out the cooler, set it up on the trunk, and invited the others to come help themselves. Why the hell was he feeling in such a rotten mood? He ought to feel great.

It was hot as hell out here—his shirt clung wetly to his back. He wasn't alone in this, he noted. Time for a little coddling for his crew. He reached into the trunk, brought out the boom box bought for rough moments with the kids.

"Okay, you guys find something you like—" He handed

the boom box to Luis, who seemed to be the leader of the three.

Mark threw together a roast beef sandwich for himself. He ate without relish, hardly conscious of the over-loud rocker that filled the air, the raucous repartee about him. He was out of prison. On his way to his first million. All of a sudden he was developing a conscience? What kind of shit was that?

He was doing the country a favor. Saving lives by putting away scum like Maglione. Only he had never got over the mental image of himself as the crusading attorney. Shove it. That was a world long lost to him.

Mark allowed a lengthy lunch break, then brought the others back to business.

"There're two parts to your training," he explained. "First you have to shoot well enough not to miss. Then you've got to learn to stage the scene right. This will be like rehearsing a play. Frank, you make the first hit. Luis, you're with him—"

In words they'd understand, Mark explained about the street scene they must enact. How it must appear natural.

"When you see the guy coming out of the building, you start arguing, loud and mad. Joey, you be the guy. Luis, you call Frank something rotten."

"You motherfucking son of a bitch!" Luis shouted with gusto. "I oughta cut off your balls!"

Mark intervened now. "Luis, when you see him pull out the gun, you go for his arm. Just touch him lightly so he can aim at the target. Don't hold his arm so he can't move it," Mark warned. "This is the action! Okay, let me see you go through it."

It was like choreographing a dance routine, Mark thought. He sat back and watched, stopped them, gave brusque instructions.

"Okay, try it again."

He interrupted again as they improved the dialogue, explained what they were doing wrong. He felt like a stage director. A Method director, he thought with ironic amusement, remembering a buddy at college who wanted to be an actor. He'd had to listen for hours to all that Method talk. The Studio, Lee Strasberg, the whole deal.

Over and over again Mark made the kids rehearse. He suspected they enjoyed the playacting. As they did so, he wrote out their improvisations.

"That's enough for today," he said finally. "Look, I'm making copies of what you kids said when you were playing the scene. You don't have to stick to it word for word, but it'll give you an idea how we have to run this show. It has to sound real," he reiterated for the dozenth time.

Chuck dropped him off at the ferry in the midst of the Friday afternoon madhouse. Onboard he listened with morbid interest to the varied conversations about him. Everybody was relieved to be escaping the torpid discomfort of the heat wave.

When the boat docked, he joined the forward surge, struggling not to stumble against valises, dodging wagons. Impatient now to be knocking at Anne's door. Forget his vow to break up what was developing—too fast—between them.

How in hell could he stay on the island and not see her?

He was hooked on Annie. And cold turkey was more than he could handle.

Chapter Fourteen

Anne was walking up from the beach when she saw Mark approaching the house.

"Hi," she called out. Her face glowed with welcome.

Mark swung about to face her. "I finished up early. I figured you might be home."

"We're having scallops in wine for dinner. You approve?" Small talk hid the questions that assaulted her mind. Why did Mark have to go into the city on a steamy day like this?

"Sounds great. I'll make the salad. That's my major culinary talent. That and dicing onions," he said and laughed.

"That'll be good. I won't have to dash around between the scallops, the sauce, and the salad."

She had not bothered to lock the door despite Doris's warning. She trailed out to the kitchen. Happy in Mark's presence. She tried to convince herself that she was happy he was here because she hated being alone in this house—but she knew better. She wouldn't look ahead, she promised herself. Take one day at a time.

She pulled out the scallops to wash, left Mark to make his choice of greens from the crisper. It felt so good having Mark here in the kitchen with her. It felt so natural. So right. She put up the scallops to simmer in the dry white wine Mark brought down for her from a top shelf. The bottle was dusty.

It had been sitting up there since last summer. Had Lila bought it to serve to one of the trail of men she entertained when Dad was in the city?

With the scallops simmering Anne reached into the refrigerator for the mushrooms, parsley, and shallots that went into the sauce.

"You've got my mushrooms," she accused Mark when she couldn't find them in the crisper.

"You expect me to leave mushrooms out of the salad when they're there for the asking?" he chided. "But here." He handed over the container. "Don't say I didn't share with you."

While she prepared the sauce, Anne talked with lively recall about the summers she'd worked on a reservation in Arizona.

"I thought then that I'd work on a reservation after college," she said. "Instead I'm up in the South Bronx. How do you know what's right?" she asked Mark with sudden intensity. "How do you know where you belong?"

"Sometimes that's decided for you." Mark's face seemed to tighten. "I know why you chose the ghetto," he decided with a move towards levity. "So you'd be close enough to spend a lot of summers at Fire Island."

"I hadn't meant to come out here this summer," Anne admitted. "But then things happened—"

"Didn't I tell you?" Mark pinpointed.

"I'm a fatalist." Sometimes she felt Mark kept a wall between them. "Everything's written out in a huge white book, and we follow what's written." Her eyes clung to his. "I think we were fated to meet—"

Mark reached to pull her to him. He kissed her with a pent-up hunger, which she reciprocated.

"Later," she said when he made a move to draw her away

from the kitchen. "After a perfect dinner, two cups of coffee, and a walk along the beach. Mark—" Her voice dropped to a whisper. "I'm so glad you came out this summer."

Anne and Mark had finished dinner and were seated on cushions before the fireplace, with coffee and Scandinavian pastries on the floor before them, when the door chimes sounded.

Anne unwound herself, rose to her feet with lifted eyebrows. "I wasn't expecting anybody," she said with faint reproach and moved to the door.

Wearing a designer pantsuit Doris waited at the door.

"Darling, I thought you might enjoy going to a party with me tonight," she said ebulliently. Her eyes lighted with approval as she spied Mark. "But I see you're busy."

Anne quickly introduced Mark and Doris.

"Stay and have coffee and dessert with us," Anne coaxed. "The party will go on forever."

"You persuaded me." Doris exuded charm. "This is a literary party. I adore writers—they're such marvelous listeners. Of course, you never know when what you've said will show up in a novel. The gal that's throwing this bash is a radical feminist. She's written a play revolving about a rape case. It's under option for production next spring." She settled herself on the sofa, accepted coffee, rejected the pastry tray. "It has a Fire Island setting, and I'd swear she's based it on Lila's rape."

Anne flinched. The idea upset her.

"Hasn't there been enough written about rape?" Mark challenged.

"That's all helped to improve the situation for women," Doris pounced. "Feminists have been damn influential in getting legislation through. Only as far back as nineteen seventy-one the state law required corroboration of penetration, identification, and lack of consent." Doris sighed. "Only three-tenths of one percent of alleged rapists were convicted. Then in nineteen seventy-two the New York State Legislature passed a new rape law that eliminated everything but corroboration of consent. Now even that's been eliminated. And if feminists can get victims to push themselves through the ugliness of the court scene, the conviction rate ought to take a real leap. God," Doris laughed, "don't I sound like I'm ready to go out and picket the men's room at P.J.Clarke's because it isn't unisexed?"

"You think this woman really used Lila's case as a basis for her play?" Anne was uncomfortable. "Isn't there a law about invasion of privacy?"

"Oh, the play will be all disguised. The idea is just the jumping-off point. Writers are forever grabbing headlines to build a play or a book on. What's more dramatic than life itself?"

"Wouldn't it be more interesting to write a play about a woman who screams rape when there was nothing at all?" Mark countered.

"That's a different approach." But Doris nodded in approval. "I'm sure there'll always be some little bitch who'll do just that. But most of the time you'd better believe the girl's been raped." Doris's eyes narrowed speculatively. "Though I was never sure about Lila."

"Doris," Anne scolded, "you just didn't like her."

"I loathed Lila," Doris conceded. "I hated the way she was cheating on your father." Her face was contrite when she saw Anne's consternation. "Darling, I didn't mean to say that. You know my big mouth. But I saw the way Lila was always picking up men and bringing them home when your father was off the island. Not to mention her big summer romance the season when she hit the headlines as the violated sub-urban matron."

"What do you mean, Doris?" Anne recoiled from dis-cussing her stepmother—yet something drove her to probe.

"That summer Lila was playing a hot and heavy scene with just one guy," Doris recalled. "He used to come over every Tuesday and Thursday on the late afternoon ferry. He went back into town the next morning. He was on the island the night of the rape."

"How can you be sure after all this time?" Mark asked.

"I remember because that afternoon I was rushing out to join a summer stock package to replace their star—she had to be shipped somewhere to be dried out. I got to the ferry too early. My watch was going berserk. And there was this char-acter getting off the incoming boat."

"Didn't you tell the cops? If her lover was here, how could she have been raped?" Mark's outrage was contagious. Anne, too, was caught up in this possible frame.

"I didn't know a damn thing about the case until I came out here the next summer," Doris explained. "After the summer tour I went straight out to the coast for a TV pilot. I didn't get back to the city until the trial was over."

"But when you found out what had happened," Mark per-sisted, "didn't you go to the police and tell them?"

"The cops would have thought I was just another actress chasing after publicity." Doris was realistic. "The man had been convicted already. A young college kid. They wouldn't have reopened the case because I said Lila Schrieber was deep in an extramarital affair. What did that have to do with the rape?" Doris glanced at her watch. She set down her mug and rose to her feet. "Maybe you two would like to come to the party?" She glanced from Mark to Anne. "No," she de-cided. "You wouldn't."

"Mark—" Anne broke the heavy silence that followed Doris's departure, "do you think it would have made any difference if it had been brought out at the trial that Lila was having an affair?"

"It would have destroyed her credibility right off," Mark pointed out. "The defense could have made good use of that."

"But if Lila wasn't raped, why would she go through that whole nasty business?" Anne was bewildered. "Why would she put Dad and herself through that?"

"To extricate herself from a difficult situation," Mark guessed. "To hide the fact that she was having an affair—"

"Doris finds drama in everything." Anne managed an indulgent smile. "Her imagination was probably working overtime." But she was disturbed. How awful if Lila *had* railroaded some innocent man into prison. "Doris admits she hated Lila." Anne forced herself to continue. "But I can't see that Lila's having an affair could have caused her to lie about the rape. Anyhow, Lila's dead. We'll never know if she lied or told the truth."

Mark walked along the deserted beach. The sky was ruddy with rain. The sea pounded at the shore. Here was where it had begun. The six-year nightmare. Right here.

Why hadn't Fremont discovered the secret affair? If Doris knew, others in the community must have known. It would have been a step towards acquittal.

Doris said the guy always stayed over until the morning. But at ten o'clock that Thursday evening Lila was screaming she had been raped.

Suddenly a vivid picture jogged into shape in Mark's mind. Lila's husband wasn't supposed to be on the island that night. She was in the sack with her lover. They heard the husband approach. The lover went out the window. Lila screamed rape and pretended to be hysterical to give him time to get away.

It could have happened like that. A vein throbbed in Mark's temple. His hands were damp with cold sweat.

Could he take this single thread that Doris had dropped into his hands and unravel the whole piece? Could he—after all these rotten years—vindicate himself? Cleared, he would be able to go to law school.

But why pursue this thread, he jeered at himself with brutal candor. He was otherwise committed. He had an operation in motion. An assignment to carry out. *And he'd been warned. There was no turning back.*

Chapter Fifteen

Mark stirred restlessly, unable to sleep. The conversation with Doris Rainey replayed itself in his mind. He could never understand Lila's pinning the rape on him. It hadn't made sense. Now he understood. Lila had pinned it on him to cover for herself and her lover. The tabloids had said she wanted to drop the charges. Her husband had insisted she go through with it.

If Doris had stayed on the island that summer, she could have helped clear him. Would she have had the guts to go to the district attorney and say, "I think you ought to know. Lila Schrieber had a lover on the island that night."

Mark turned this over in his mind. If Doris had been here, she would have acted. If he managed to get the case reopened, would she repeat to the DA what she had said last night at Anne's house?

What's the matter with me? That slim thread, at this late date, isn't enough to get me past the DA's third assistant.

But what if he pursued that fragile thread himself? His heart began to pound. His mind charged into high gear. Think like a lawyer. Look at the case from every angle.

Suppose he could come up with more? If he could nail Lila's lover, corner him, drag him to the DA with an admission that he had been in Lila's bed that night, they would have to reopen the case! *So I've served my sentence. I want to clear my name.*

He was conscious of a surge of exhilaration. If he was cleared of the rape charge, he wouldn't be a felon. He could go to law school—even at this late date. He could come out of school and practice law, live the life he'd planned for himself a dozen years ago. A life that could include Anne.

What the hell is the matter with me? I've already crossed to the other side of the road. I have a contract to fulfill.

He could hear Brooks's steel-edged voice. "You take on an assignment, we expect the job to be done. You talk about repercussions, Forrest. Fail and you'll know what that means." If Maglione wasn't snuffed out, *he* was as good as dead.

Mark switched on his bedside lamp, went out to the kitchen to put up coffee. The whole nightmare trial was ablaze in his mind again. The procession of witnesses for Lila. Fremont's understated cross-examination that did nothing to help the case. Mom, always sitting in the first row of spectators, so sure he'd be cleared. Still believing in the great judicial system.

Everybody insisted he had no grounds for an appeal. Maybe now he could come up with some grounds. He had a lead. Private investigators came high, but a chunk of the money from the Long Island house was in that joint account for him to use when he needed it.

But he couldn't erase the one deadly problem that stared him in the face. If he didn't go through with his deal with Brooks, if he failed to eliminate Maglione, there would be a contract out on him.

The coffee was perking. Mark poured himself a cup, walked with it into the bedroom, sprawled on the bed. How could he not act, knowing what he knew now? His expensive, stupid lawyer! Why hadn't he dug up the dirt on Lila Schrieber?

He ordered himself to focus on the situation. Think it through clearly. He had accepted no money yet from Brooks, he reminded himself with a flicker of optimism. The first payment was due when the date was arranged.

Oh, cut the crap—he was acting like a kid. Nothing had changed. He'd spent six years in prison for a crime he didn't commit. Only now he knew why he had been screwed.

His life from this point on was marked out for him. He played in the same field as Brooks. Chuck was his man, those punk kids his staff. But he'd live well. Better than Mark Cameron, attorney, would have lived. But that wasn't enough—

He switched off the lamp and lay back against the pillow. Willing himself to sleep. But he was as wide awake as if it were mid-afternoon. He thrashed about on the bed—seeking a position that would be conducive to sleep.

After twenty minutes he conceded it was useless to try to sleep. *Throw on some clothes, go down to the beach.* In sneakers, jeans, T-shirt and windbreaker he walked out of the house and down to the broad avenue of sand. A dank cold enveloped him as he walked. He ignored the drizzle that began to fall.

A pup—probably no more than four or five months old—came towards him and fell in step. He stooped to fondle the beige fur that covered a too-lean frame. Bright intelligent eyes. No collar. He wasn't lost, Mark realized. He'd been abandoned.

At the dock Mark saw a cluster of fishermen heading for a boat.

"This your dog?" he called out.

"Not ours," one of the group answered. "Is there a name on the license tag?"

"No license tag, no collar," Mark said.

"Some bastard came out for the day and dumped him," another of the group surmised. "That happens every now and then."

"Too often," another grumbled.

The pup shivered. Mark reached down to pick him up. The poor little character looked half-starved. With the dog in his arms he left the pier and headed for home. By the time he approached the door, the rain was hammering at his shoulders.

Mark took the pup out to the kitchen, deposited him on the floor while he checked his meagerly supplied refrigerator. He opened a package of cold cuts, pulled out three slices, ripped them into bite-sized portions and put them on a plate.

He felt less alone as he watched the pup devour the food. He brought out more cold cuts from the refrigerator, poured milk into a bowl. He'd put up a note at the pier in the morning in case the little guy was lost.

With the dog bedded down at his feet and rain beating on the roof, Mark eventually fell asleep again. By the time he awoke, it was early afternoon. The puppy was immediately alert, avid for play. Last night's rain had dissipated. Sunlight poured onto the bed.

Mark allowed himself a few minutes of good-humored tussling with the pup, then went in to shower—leaving the door open so his tiny houseguest didn't feel shut out.

He emerged from the shower to find the pup sprawled in the doorway.

"I'll bet you're hungry again," he crooned while he dried himself. He'd shave later. "Let me get on swimming trunks and we'll see about breakfast."

Heading for the kitchen, he recognized a sudden urgency in his companion. With an understanding grin he opened the back door, leaving it propped wide with a garbage pail.

In minutes the pup returned, settled at Mark's feet while he put up coffee and prepared himself scrambled eggs and toast. As an afterthought he added more eggs. Instinct told him this little character would eat anything edible put before him.

He ate with little relish while his companion slurped scrambled eggs with obvious appreciation. He lingered at the table over a second cup of coffee. He would have been better off if he had never met Doris Rainey, he told himself with frustration. Before then he was sure of his direction. Now his mind was in chaos.

All at once the pup began to bark. He chased from the kitchen to the front door. Someone must have knocked. The bell wasn't working, he remembered now.

"Hi—" Anne's voice trickled to Mark as he walked towards the door, pulled it wide. His head was pounding. "So you've acquired a friend."

"I found him on the beach." Mark realized he sounded abnormally impersonal. He didn't want to see Anne right now. He wasn't ready to come to grips with reality. "I'll have to put up a notice and wait for somebody to claim him." He forced a smile as he pushed the screen door open for her. "Come in and have some coffee."

"I was on my way to the grocery store." Anne walked inside. Her smile was uncertain. *She senses I'm in a rotten mood.*

"Come in and have coffee anyway." He tried to sound casual.

"Are you keeping the pup if nobody claims him?" Anne bent to pat his head.

"Probably." Sure, he'd keep the little character. All at once he felt an intense loyalty towards the dog. "Annie, meet Hannibal." The name chosen at that moment.

"Hello, Hannibal." She dropped to her haunches to pet

him, laughed as he lathered her with ecstatic kisses. "Yes, you're a terrific baby—"

Anne followed Mark into the kitchen, stayed only long enough to have a cup of coffee with him. Their conversation was strained. *Anne looks hurt. She can't figure me out. Why can't I act normal?*

"I'm sorry I'm such lousy company," he apologized, walking with her to the door. "I slept forever—woke up with a rotten headache."

"Try some fresh air." She pretended to be flip. He knew she was upset. "I'll see you." It was a dismissal of a beginning relationship. "So long, Hannibal. See you, too."

Mark tried a cold shower. It cleared his head a bit. He checked his watch. It was time to go to the pier to phone Chuck at the pool hall. First he wrote out a notice about Hannibal and took it over to tape up on the bulletin board near the pier.

He had to wait a few minutes for a phone. He swore under his breath as the coins in his hand fell to the floor. He retrieved them, put through the call. Chuck was waiting.

"Yeah?" Chuck seemed in high spirits.

"Okay, what's the score?" Mark asked.

"I worked with the kids all mornin', then drove them back to town and—"

"How're they doing?" Mark asked. The schedule called for Chuck to pick up the kids at eight a.m. sharp, drive out to the shooting area, put them through target practice for four hours, then drive them back into the South Bronx. "Think they can handle the deal?"

"You don't expect them to be winning sharpshooter prizes." Chuck was defensive. "At close range they're already okay. And they're dyin' for action."

"What about Brooks?" Mark asked.

"Like you told me, I phoned Brooks. I spoke to one of his creepy 'associates.' He said I could pick up the photos Monday mornin'." *So nothing happens over the weekend.* "And he said to tell you word is around that Maglione will be in town before next weekend."

"Good." But Mark flinched at this. There was no good way out of the situation he'd created.

"You want I should make a quick trip out to the island?" Chuck sounded doubtful. "I couldn't do much more than grab three or four hours' sleep. I gotta be back to pick up the young creeps at eight tomorrow morning," he reminded.

"No," Mark dismissed this, his mind charging ahead. Forming a desperate plan. "No sense in that. I'm coming into the city." Maglione would be in town by next weekend. A date would be set. He'd collect half of their fee. Why didn't he feel jubilant? "If I rush, I can make the next ferry to Bay Shore." He juggled time in his head. "I should be in the city about four-thirty this afternoon. No, that's pushing it." He had another destination before he met Chuck. "Meet me around six p.m. At the OTB windows in Grand Central. Okay?"

"Sure thing, Boss—" Chuck couldn't figure out why he was coming into the city today.

Mark charged back to the house, was greeted joyously by Hannibal. What would he do about the little guy? he asked himself in alarm. Let him out for a couple of minutes, leave more cold cuts. So he'd make it back on the last ferry. Hannibal would be all right here in the house till then.

He allowed Hannibal a two-minute run out back, brought him into the house again, locked up and charged towards the dock. He'd make the ferry, he told himself with a blend of desperation and jubilation. Intent on being in the city by 4:30 p.m.

The ferry was boarding as he arrived. He jumped onboard with a sigh of relief. On a Friday afternoon people were coming out—few going in. He stood at the railing and fought to bring order out of the chaos in his mind.

Fremont's offices were on Fifth Avenue just above Forty-second Street. He would drop in and pay his respects to his former lawyer. And ask some loaded questions. He wasn't sure where he would go with the answers.

The Fire Island vacation wasn't working out, he taunted himself. He'd move back to the city, stay at the apartment. Those final weeks in prison he'd clung to the prospect of a few weeks at the house on Fire Island. But then he'd met Annie, and his world was turned upside down. This whole scene wasn't fair to her.

I could tell Annie who I am. That would cut off the relationship fast enough! There's nothing ahead for us.

Why had he allowed that little talk with Doris Rainey to rock him this way? To give him hopes of a new life? He'd smashed all hopes when he made his business deal with Brooks. He'd met Annie—and Doris—too late.

As he'd anticipated, the city wore the air of a mass exodus. His heart pounding, he rushed to the skyscraper where Fremont maintained a lush suite of offices. He arrived in the lobby as masses of employees were emerging from the bank of elevators. Lively chatter about weekend plans. The past week had been a scorcher in the city.

He waited impatiently for the elevator to be clear, strode inside, rode up to the twenty-third floor. Striving for an air of calm, he hurried from the elevator, walked with an air of un-reality to the entrance to Fremont's suite. No lights shone from within. The door was locked.

Shouldn't he have known that Fremont had probably been on the road out of town by ten yesterday morning? Half the city was already on the three-day summer weekend routine. He'd have to wait until Monday to pursue this madness.

He walked aimlessly about the city. He was to meet Chuck at 6:00 p.m. Why? he asked himself. Chuck must think he was off the wall. Okay, tell him he came into New York to check some facts about Maglione in the New York Public Library microfilm files. Chuck would understand that.

He'd make that trip to the library on Monday. Be prepared if Maglione arrived in town early in the week. The research was important. He'd buy Chuck a fancy dinner, and he'd be happy. Then he'd head back to Bay Shore for the ferry to the island.

Chuck would work with the kids over the weekend, stay at the apartment. A beach house was not his thing. On Monday around noon they'd meet at their usual place—the Grand Central OTB. Monday Chuck would bring him the snapshots of Maglione.

Sometime Monday he'd call on Fremont. Ask questions.

Chapter Sixteen

Mark was determined to sleep away the weekend. Not to succumb and go to Annie's house. No, he mocked himself, Lila Schrieber's house. To him it would always be Lila Schrieber's house. The beginning of the end for him.

On Saturday he slept till past noon. Now he lay awake in bed, reluctant to face the world, his mind assaulted by images of Annie. She was baffled. She couldn't figure out what had gone wrong for them. They were great together in all the important ways. Except that her stepmother had screwed him royally. Correction—he was supposed to have screwed her stepmother.

He made breakfast, fed Hannibal, let him out for a brief run—knowing he'd return to his one safe haven. He made an effort to watch TV, zeroed in on CNN. Much talk about the Supreme Court's reaffirming rights to abortion. More talk about the coming Democratic convention. He was betting that Clinton—the former Arkansas governor—would be their candidate. Much talk about the Labor Party winning the June 23 election in Israel.

At the approach of evening—restless, harried—he decided he'd go to the movie. Hannibal complained briefly at being closed up in the house. Halfway down the block Mark returned to light a lamp for him. It would be dark by the time the first feature was over.

Mark walked to the low, white building that housed the theater, bought a ticket without bothering to notice what was playing. When the film began, he struggled to become involved.

Instead, his mind focused on the possibilities opened up by Doris's disclosure of Lila Schrieber's extramarital affair. But what would be the use of following up on this?

Leaving the movie he paused to buy an ice-cream cone, not bothering to acknowledge the good-humored invitation of a pair of tight-jeaned, halter-topped teenagers among the nightwalkers. He returned to the house to a joyous reception by Hannibal, who was delighted to finish off the ice cream.

"Okay, let's go to the beach." He felt guilty that Hannibal had been housebound so long.

He'd have to buy a leash. He'd look for a vet to give Hannibal his shots. Anybody who abandoned a pup would have hardly attended to such niceties.

Walking down the narrow path to the night-darkened beach, he made an effort to keep his eyes averted from the Schrieber house. Fog was rolling in from the sea. One faint light was visible in the distance. He walked slowly, Hannibal at his heels, until he saw a night party ahead. Abruptly he turned back.

Walking up the stairs from the beach he was faced with a splash of lights in Anne's glass-rich living room. His face tightened. He would not go to Annie.

"Hannibal!" he called out in irritation because the pup was chasing after a calico cat just a few yards ahead. "Hannibal! Get back here!"

He caught up with Hannibal, who paused in indignation that the cat had outdistanced him and was beyond view. Mark smacked him lightly on the rump.

"No chasing cats, you hear?" He was conscious of the spill

of lights in Anne's ocean-facing house, and he knew at this moment that—despite his determination to stay away—he would go to her.

Her face lighted as she opened the door.

"Hi."

All at once he was uncomfortable. *Why had he come?* "Busy?"

"No. Come in, Mark." Her eyes searched his. She sensed he was fighting some inner conflict. Yet he knew she wouldn't probe.

"I'm sorry I was so rotten yesterday. I've got some problems to work out." He trailed into the house with Hannibal at his heels. "Is it okay if Hannibal comes inside?"

"Mark," she clucked in reproach.

He walked into the living room and dropped onto the sofa.

"I went to the movies." He shook his head tiredly. "Annie, I'm on a roller coaster, and I can't jump off."

"Do you want to talk about it?" She sat at the corner of the sofa and tucked her legs beneath her. Hannibal settled himself at her feet and lifted his head to be fondled.

"I can't talk about it." *I shouldn't have come here.*

"Hungry?" she asked after a moment.

"I had a burger a couple of hours ago."

"Come out to the kitchen. I make the best quick spaghetti with meat sauce you ever tangled with."

In the kitchen Anne went about preparing the spaghetti. She ordered Mark to handle the salad. She flipped on the radio.

"Breaking up is hard to do—" Neil Sedaka's voice filled the room. An oldie he'd always liked.

A coldness closed in about Mark. He didn't want to break up with Anne.

They ate in the kitchen. Hannibal accepted spaghetti but

rejected the salad. Mark insisted on cleaning up. They both knew how the evening would end. When he had put away the last dish and washed the counter, he turned around to see Anne standing in the doorway in a beach robe. He knew she was naked underneath.

They locked Hannibal out of the bedroom and made love. It was great. The way it had been before. They lay beneath a light blanket now, legs tangled together, knowing in a little while they'd make love again. The scent of the sea permeated the darkness. Beyond the door Hannibal snored.

"That was a way-out story about your stepmother that Doris brought up last night," he said after a moment of silence between them.

"I've been thinking about it." She was somber. "Could Lila have lied? It doesn't make sense."

"According to Doris, Lila was—very promiscuous."

"She was a bitch," Anne said passionately. "I saw her myself, when I was fifteen—coming out of a motel unit with a man. Oh, I knew the gossip about the men she met in bars. Doris wasn't making up that bit about the summer romance." Anne's eyes were troubled. "Mark, how awful if some innocent boy went to jail because Lila lied in court."

Here it was. The moment to tell her. Mark trembled. His mouth went dry. But the words refused to come. Not yet. He couldn't tell her yet. Instead, he reached to pull her to him again.

Chapter Seventeen

Mark woke up with a sense of plummeting through space. He heard Hannibal whimpering outside the bedroom door. Instantly he was conscious that he had spent the night in Lila Schrieber's house. He turned to Anne. She was fast asleep, her face burrowed in the pillow. One slim foot dangled over the side of the bed.

He left the bed, went to let Hannibal out for the necessary few moments. By the time he had dressed and walked out to the kitchen, Hannibal was asking to come back in. He opened the door for Hannibal, crossed to the chalkboard Anne kept for grocery reminders.

He had to do this, he ordered himself. Before Annie was deeply hurt. He printed a message for her. In block letters so there could be no mistake.

See you, Annie, when I get my head together.

"Come on, Hannibal," he said with unintentional harshness that elicited a glint of surprise. "Let's go home." This time his voice was gentle.

He spent the rest of the day holed up in his house. He didn't even bother to try to pick up a copy of the Sunday *Times*, which had been a ritual other summers on the island. But this wasn't like the other summers.

He ate, with Hannibal, from what remained in the refrigerator. In the morning, before he took the ferry, he'd go to buy some canned dog food. Not too many cans. He wasn't going to spend the rest of the summer out here. How could he live a few houses away from Annie and not be with her?

It was crazy to pursue Fremont, but he *had* to ask some questions. Even though he knew it wouldn't change a thing, he had to ask. Fremont would be back in the office tomorrow—after a three-day weekend at the Hamptons or the Cape. Fire Island wasn't his style.

He'd walk in without phoning. Catch him by surprise. A cynical smile touched his face. A hundred to one Fremont wouldn't even be back in town on Monday. Lawyers in his category were prone to four-day weekends during the summer.

He was conscious of figures passing the house. Each time he stiffened in anticipation. Half-expecting, half-hoping Annie would drop by. Not likely, though, after the message he'd left. She was too sensitive to intrude when he made it clear he wanted to be alone.

Hell, he didn't want to be alone. He wanted to turn the calendar back seven years.

Mark went to bed early, rose early. He showered, dressed, went to the grocery to buy dog food. He fed Hannibal, left dry dog food and a bowl of water for him. He wouldn't be back on the island until evening.

He checked the ferry schedule. He'd miss the mad hassle of the early Monday morning ferry. He wasn't in the mood to share the air of conviviality that was part of the Monday morning trek back to the city.

Once aboard the ferry Mark stayed at the railing all the way to the mainland. He rejected the waiting cabs bound for the train into Manhattan. He had another destination before he took the train.

It was time to go to the bank where Mom kept a safe deposit box in both their names. The deed to the house was there, along with insurance papers and some jewelry that had belonged to his grandmother. Today he must switch to a larger box. To handle Brooks's cash payment.

He found a cab to take him to the bank. He took care of his business there, called for a cab to take him to the train. On the commuter run to Manhattan he focused on reading the morning's edition of the *New York Times*. The moment the train moved underground—signaling its imminent arrival in Penn Station—he was on his feet.

At last out of the Monday morning madness of Penn Station, he walked north to Forty-second Street in the sweltering sunlight. Already his shirt clung damply between his shoulder blades.

With luck he'd catch Fremont in his office. This was an absurd but obsessive mission. He had to face Fremont and ask questions.

"Why didn't you find out that Lila Schrieber was promiscuous? Why did you let the prosecution set her up as the Westchester clubwoman deep in the philanthropic scene? Why didn't you know about the lover who was there on the island that night?"

At Forty-second Street he turned east, walked rapidly past the block dedicated to sex films, massage parlors, and—incongruously—a chess house. As he waited for the traffic light to change from red to green at Times Square, he visualized the insane New Year's Eve when a dozen Long Island teenagers—including himself—had piled into two cars to be part of the crowd that waited for that ball to fall at the stroke of midnight.

He continued east, caught up in the past. The main New York Public Library at the corner of Fifth Avenue. God, the

121

hours he'd spent inside those walls working on papers when he was in Stuyvesant High. Sometimes Room 315 seemed his second home.

As he neared Fifth Avenue, Mark grew more tense. Fremont's office was minutes away. He hadn't seen the attorney since his conviction. Now the memory of those ghastly days tickertaped across his mind. *Let Fremont be there today.*

He walked into the lobby of the skyscraper that housed Fremont's suite of offices, waited before the bank of elevators. The express elevator zoomed with silent speed down to the lobby. The door swung open. Mark moved inside. Moments later the lightly populated car shot upwards.

The elevator slid to a stop at his floor. Mark emerged, walked along the hallway with instant recall of the locale of Fremont's office. The pair of double doors at the far end to the right. He wanted Fremont to be in his office. He had been paid enough to extend the courtesy of one more consultation.

In the smartly furnished reception room the woman at the desk lifted her head from a paperback to smile pleasantly at him. She was middle-aged, stiffly coiffed, well-dressed. There'd been a young redhead with fantastically long hair when he was seeing Fremont while out on bail.

"Is Mr. Fremont in the office?" Mark was conscious of a pain in his gut. He felt as though he was about to go on trial again.

"Do you have an appointment?" Reservation in her smile now.

"Please tell Mr. Fremont that Mark Cameron is here," he said briskly. "I'm an old client."

The receptionist called Fremont's office, then turned to Mark again.

"You'll find Mr. Fremont in the second office to the left. Go right in, please."

As Mark entered the large, square, tastefully decorated office, Fremont rose from his desk and extended a hand in welcome.

"Mark, good to see you." He was effusive, yet Mark sensed a wariness in him. No lawyer enjoys meeting a client he's allowed to serve time. "How long have you been out?" He could not completely mask his self-consciousness.

"Not long." Mark battled an instinct to run.

"How's your mother?" Fremont was curious about his being there.

"She's fine. She's married again, you know. They're living down in Rio for a while." Stop this chitchat. Get down to business. "Mr. Fremont, I'm staying out on Fire Island for a while. The locale of my case," he amplified. Fremont had tried a lot of cases since his. "I've run into a situation that's bugging me."

"What kind of a situation?" Suddenly Fremont was shuffling papers into a briefcase.

"I discovered that Lila Schrieber had a lover that summer. He came out to the island—without fail—every Tuesday and Thursday afternoon. Mr. Fremont, I was accused of raping Lila Schrieber on a Thursday evening."

"So he missed that Thursday." Fremont was irritated.

"No, he did not miss that Thursday," Mark said with quiet conviction. "Lila's husband came back unexpectedly. Lila was in the sack with her lover. He went out the window and Lila screamed rape, played hysterical to give him time to clear out. Mr. Fremont, if we can track down Lila Schrieber's lover, I can be cleared of the rape charge."

"Mark, you've served your time." Fremont was testy.

"I'm thinking about my name!"

"We can't get the case reopened." Fremont was impatient. "Lila's lover isn't going to testify in your behalf. Certainly she won't."

"Lila died in a car accident months ago," Mark brushed this aside. "But I have a witness who'll testify that the lover was on the island that night. She saw him get off the ferry that Thursday afternoon."

"Which takes you nowhere. Mark, forget it. It was a rotten break. I never expected the judge to be so heavy."

"You never believed I was innocent!" Mark exploded. "All you cared about was getting as short a sentence as possible. It didn't matter that I was being railroaded!"

"The evidence was stacked against you." Fremont was detached. "I didn't know whether you were guilty or not. I gave you the best possible defense. Nobody could do more than that."

"You made no effort to discredit Lila Schrieber's credibility. You didn't look for a possible lover." Rage ricocheted in his voice. "You were so damn sure I was guilty you didn't try."

"I said I didn't know if you were guilty." Fremont refused to abandon his detachment. "I had a man at the island asking questions about her background. He came up with nothing."

"Now we have something," Mark pinpointed. "What do you propose to do about it?"

"You have nothing to go on," Fremont countered. "Some gossipy neighbor making accusations against a woman who's dead. Now if you'll excuse me, I have to leave for court." He paused. "Mark, forget it. You've served your time. You're free. Learn to live again."

"Wow, that's beautiful," Mark said scathingly. "An ex-con looking for a place in society. You know what's open to me. If I can reverse the conviction—"

"No chance." Fremont was cold. "Now you must excuse me." He kept his eyes averted. "I have to leave for court."

White with fury Mark strode from the office. He hadn't

planned on an ugly confrontation with Fremont. What had he planned? he asked himself bluntly. He wasn't thinking straight. He was acting on impulse. Fremont was right, he forced himself to acknowledge. At this point he didn't have enough to reopen the case. *Can I come up with more?*

He glanced at his watch. He had over an hour to kill before he met Chuck. Find an elegant Madison Avenue restaurant and go in for a long, expensive lunch. Then back to Grand Central to meet Chuck. The three kids were off today—Chuck was picking up the snapshots of Maglione and bringing them to him.

After the meeting with Chuck he'd go do some research in Room 315 at the main public library. They'd have the newspapers on microfilm. He must make sure the contract was on a hood. It wasn't enough to have Chuck's okay.

Over a satisfying luncheon Mark found himself reliving that brief encounter with Fremont. He knew deep inside that he didn't have enough to reopen the case.

How can I dig in and get stronger evidence to clear myself?

Chapter Eighteen

A paperback in one hand, Anne walked out of the house and onto the deck, lowered herself onto one of the pair of chaises that sat under the awning area. She dropped the paperback on the table beside the chaise, gazed at the ocean without seeing. The note Mark had left was upsetting. She knew he was in some kind of emotional turmoil. Why couldn't he share it with her?

Almost from the first evening, she had known he was troubled. Why had he left the farm? Had he been through a bad love affair? Was that why he didn't trust what was happening between them? How could she help him? He wouldn't let her, she tormented herself. He was putting up a wall between them.

With a sigh of frustration she reached for the paperback, opened it to where she'd placed the bookmark. She tried to involve herself in the novel. Her mind rebelled. After a few sentences she closed the book and returned it to the table. Without Mark the hours dragged. She had come out to the island with such anticipation. Eager to escape the frenzy at the office, the city heat, the crowds. At unwary moments she worried about Joey—adrift in the South Bronx.

She didn't have to be lonely, she rebuked herself. It was easy to make friends on the beach. There were families here whom she had known since Dad bought the house. There was

Doris. She couldn't sit out the summer, waiting for Mark to get his head together.

She remembered she needed some things at the grocery. That was something to do. And on the way back, she'd stop by and see if Doris was home.

She went inside, changed from swimsuit to shorts and top. She found a floppy hat to protect her face from the sun, slid her feet into thonged sandals. Mark hadn't come down to the beach this morning as she had hoped he would. He had not come down because he knew she would be there.

She left the house, headed for the grocery store, conscious that the house where Mark was staying was just ahead. He wasn't sharing. Probably the two of them were the only ones in the community staying alone in a house. This was the era of "shares."

She should have rented the house for the summer. It was a mad extravagance to use it just for herself. But she wanted to be out here alone this summer. To remember the great summers with Dad—before Lila.

She passed Mark's house—conscious of its air of desertion. Was Mark down on the beach, looking for somebody new? Or had he gone into New York or Bay Shore on one of those errands he never explained?

Was Mark job hunting? He'd talked vaguely about going back to law school. Maybe he was pressed for money. *I could help him through law school. The money's coming in now from Dad's estate. Lots of wives help their husbands through graduate school. But I'm not Mark's wife.*

Anne shopped for a few items in the grocery store, inspected slacks in a shop window, discarded the idea of going inside to try them on. She wasn't in the mood today.

She walked past Mark's house again, subconsciously slowing her steps. Whatever his problem, why couldn't he share it with her? There were beautiful moments when they felt so close.

In a corner of her mind she tried to bring together the facts she knew about Mark. In truth, so little. Only the business about cutting out of college and living on the farm commune. His father was dead, his mother remarried. When he talked about his mother, he showed deep affection for her.

She knew how Mark felt about the environment, politics, ecology, the legal system. She knew the kind of music he liked and his taste in reading. He had astonished her with his knowledge of sociopathy. Still, that wasn't much to know about a man with whom she wished to share the rest of her life.

As she approached Doris's house, she heard the stentorian tones of a Wagnerian opera. Doris was an opera buff. Anne rang the bell, then knocked because it was hardly likely Doris would hear the delicate chimes of the doorbell over the music.

Wearing one of her exotic caftans, Doris came to the door.

"Darling, am I glad to see you. I simply wasn't in the mood for opera this afternoon." She pulled the door wide, beckoned Anne inside with a radiant smile. "I'll make us wine coolers and we'll sit and rap." She paused to turn off the CD player. "We'll sit out on the deck. It's damn hot indoors without air-conditioning—even with the breeze."

They lingered in the kitchen while Doris prepared the coolers in tall Danish glasses, then moved out to the deck.

"How's that gorgeous young man I met at your house on Friday?" Doris's eyes were bright with interest. "I liked him on sight. I always trust my instincts about people."

"Mark's fine," Anne said with a casual smile. Doris wouldn't probe. "How was your party the other night?"

"Great. You two should have come," she said enthusiastically. "Jeannie had arranged for a reading of a new play. There should be a part in it for me."

"Oh, wonderful!" Doris had been uneasy at being idle.

"Not the lead," Doris conceded with a wry smile, "but something small and spectacular. You remember, I told you it was about a rape case."

"Right—" Anne nodded.

"Only this isn't the conventional rape case. It's a frame. Not at all what I would have expected from an ardent women's libber like Jeannie Walters, but it makes for terrific theater."

"A fresh approach—"

Doris leaned forward, caught up in the momentum of the play. "The woman is middle-aged, glamorous, but scared to death of losing her looks and her men. She's having a mad summer romance with somebody fifteen years younger. She's in bed with him when her husband suddenly appears at the door of the house. He wasn't due until the last ferry on Friday night. The lover beats it out through the window, and she pulls the rape bit to cover while he clears out. She picks some kid out of a line-up, swears he raped her. At the last minute, when the jury's all ready to go out, the girl who he insists was with him all evening, shows up to clear him. She'd been in Europe all through the trial."

"Doris, do you believe something like that happened with Lila?" Anne's voice was uneven. "Did Lila frame that man?" It was sick if that happened.

"It could have been that way." Doris nodded, caught up in the drama of the situation.

"Did Jeannie Walters know Lila?" Anne pushed. Her mind racing.

"They'd met at a few parties. Reading about the trial, Jeannie's writer's mind took off," she said. "Jeannie doesn't know anything," she emphasized with honesty, suspecting the questions that were assailing Anne. "Somebody who had been out here that summer tried to pin her down," Doris recalled.

"What did she say?" Did Lila do this awful thing?

"Jeannie admitted she knew about the rape case, of course—and she decided Fire Island was a sensational setting. She let her imagination go to work, and the play developed."

"It could have happened that way," Anne said slowly. "Doris, we ought to try to track down that man. Find out who was his attorney. He may be in jail now because Lila lied!"

"Darling, we don't *know* that she did," Doris pointed out. "My suspicions may be completely crazy. Anyway, Lila's dead. There's no way to find out who the character was that she was sleeping with that summer. I hope to God, though, that the man in the case wasn't framed."

Chapter Nineteen

Mark lingered in the lush air-conditioning of the restaurant, along with a few expense-account diners taking the long lunch. He was still uptight from the encounter with Fremont. The rotten bastard! Fremont didn't give a damn that his life had been turned upside down. Case closed. Fremont had been paid. Screw it.

Mark checked his watch. It was still early. He recoiled from the prospective meeting with Chuck. Chuck would give him the snaps of Maglione. He would go to the library, check him out via microfilm of back issues of the Times and a bunch of news magazines. It was only to confirm what he already knew. Maglione was a hood. How many times had Maglione killed?

What would Anne think if she knew about his new career? She would be revolted. How could she feel otherwise? He was using those sociopaths she was trying to save. He was preparing to become a killer. So he didn't pull the trigger. He would be the engineer.

He glanced about the dining room. It was growing empty. A waiter came forward as he reached for his wallet. No credit cards, he thought wryly. That would surprise the waiter. Later he'd figure out a way to acquire them.

His mind charged back to those years in prison. He'd collected an odd assortment of knowledge. What one lifer—hoping for early parole—had called street smarts. He could hear his voice now, raspy and defiant:

"You gotta build yourself a whole new identification. And you can do it. You can buy almost anything on the streets. Once you have a new Social Security number—but make sure the first three numbers code the state where you got the card—you're on your way."

He'd chosen his new name for the outside world over a year ago. He'd vowed to come out of prison and buy himself a life of good things, to make up for what the judicial system had done to him. That was how he survived, he told himself yet again. But now he felt sick about what lay ahead. What happened to his head in those miserable years?

His waiter came to the table—startled that he offered a fifty-dollar bill rather than a credit card.

"I left my credit cards in another wallet," he alibied and scolded himself for this subterfuge.

He waited for his change, tipped heavily, and went out into the hot, bright sunlight. He walked slowly down Madison Avenue to Forty-second Street and swung east. The OTB windows in the cavernous core of Grand Central were doing a healthy business. Chuck had not yet arrived.

Mark walked down to a stand-up lunch counter and ordered orange juice, perspiring in the sultry heat. He had just drained the glass when he saw Chuck saunter into view. He put down the glass, strode to where Chuck stood gazing about with self-conscious uncertainty.

"Did you have any trouble parking?" he asked and Chuck grinned in relief.

"I had to go over to Second Avenue. The creeps are waitin' in the car."

"I thought you were giving them today off?" A mild reproach in Mark's voice.

"I was, but they weren't happy." Chuck grinned. "They

want that ten bucks a day 'expense money.' " He fished in his pocket, pulled forth an envelope. "Here are the snaps of Maglione. They're all from just a few months ago."

"Good." Mark opened the envelope, pulled out a bunch of snapshots.

"Brooks wants you to call him after you've checked out Maglione. He'll be at the Long Island house all day. He'll tell you when Maglione's due in and where he'll be stayin'. You work out the schedule with him." Chuck's eyes glinted with anticipation. He was mentally spending his share of the first contract.

"The punks behaving themselves? They're not spilling their guts on the street?" Mark's main worry.

"Are you kiddin'?" Chuck jeered. "With that loot on the line? They don't let out a peep."

"How're they handling themselves? I want to see them in action later in the week."

"They'll be like graduates," Chuck bragged. "They can shoot almost as good as me. And wow, they drink up that playactin'. You'd think they were auditionin' for a part on 'Law & Order.' "

"I'm going to the library now," Mark told him. "Forget taking the crew for a workout today. Give them the ten-buck 'expense money' and take them home. Meet me at the pool hall in two hours. And don't get fancy on the road. That car has to hold up until I buy myself a Jaguar." *I don't need a Jaguar. I need a normal life. I need Annie in my life.*

Chuck headed back for the car. Mark took off in the opposite direction. At the Forty-second Street library he went up to the third floor, into the area where the microfilms were available. All he needed was one item to confirm that Tony Maglione was a gangland figure. Instinct told him that wouldn't be hard to come by.

It took Mark only an hour to find everything he wanted. Not just one confirming article—a dozen. No doubt about it. Maglione was into hard drugs and prostitution. He had been in and out of the courts. No convictions, but his hands were bloody. Plus Brooks's crowd was certain he'd killed Brooks's nephew.

Mark walked down the marble-floored third-story hall to the elevators. Chuck said he was to call Brooks some time today. Did Brooks have definite information about Maglione's arrival in the city? He wouldn't pass that along through Chuck. Brooks would give that information directly to him.

The third-floor phones were all occupied. He'd try the phones downstairs. Waiting for the elevator he fished Brooks's home phone number from his wallet. Damn, he couldn't walk out on the deal with Brooks! The old boy had been explicit about what would happen if Maglione wasn't hit.

Damn Fremont! He should have shown some interest. He knew a sharp PI could track down Lila's lover. With that information—and Doris Rainey's testimony—Fremont would have grounds to ask that the case be reopened.

On the Forty-second Street level of the library Mark went to the phones. One was available. He put through the call to Brooks. The maid answered. In moments Brooks was on the other end.

"Yes?"

"Maglione checks out," Mark said crisply. "When's he due in the city?"

"Friday. He'll be staying at his family's house in the Bay Ridge section of Brooklyn. Know the neighborhood?"

"I'll give it a dry run," Mark promised. "What's the address?"

Brooks gave him the address of the house. He repeated it carefully as Mark wrote in his notebook.

"Got it," Mark assured him.

"He's going to a wedding on Saturday at three o'clock. Write down the name of the church."

"Go ahead," Mark ordered and wrote down the additional information. "Where does he go from the wedding? Will there be a reception?"

"Yeah, here's the place—"

It would be a fancy Italian wedding. He would plan for the punks to nail Maglione as he went into the reception. There would be a lot of people around. It would look like a crazy accident. But even as he outlined the way to handle the hit, he was repelled. *How did I get myself into this? It was my way of surviving those years in prison.*

"You got everything straight?" Brooks demanded.

"Everything," Mark reassured him. His head pounded now.

"No slip-ups, Forrest," Brooks warned.

"I like your confidence," Mark drawled. "Have the money ready on Wednesday at eleven. Fifty percent of the deal. Nothing larger than hundreds. I'll be there with my man." A stranger was talking with his voice. He was playing a role he wanted to abdicate.

"That's a big advance," Brooks complained. "I don't like it."

"Mr. Brooks, your money goes into a safe deposit box. It stays there until I collect the second payment." This was what he had planned, fought to bring to reality. "My word, Mr. Brooks."

"Your word?" Brooks mocked.

"I'm a new breed," Mark shot back. "I stick to my word. Have the money ready," he repeated. "Wednesday at eleven."

Chapter Twenty

Mark walked from the ferry in the comfortable coolness of the island night, shoulders hunched, impatient to be out of his clothes and standing beneath a hot shower to wash away the perspiration embedded in his skin.

He ached to escape from the memory of those heated minutes in Fremont's office. Absurdly, he had hoped Fremont would come up with positive answers. He wanted to forget the contract he must fulfill to stay alive. He wanted to make love to Annie.

Approaching the house he was startled to see a light on in the kitchen. He frowned as he mentally reconstructed his activities that morning. He had not left on the light. What the hell had happened? Anxiety for Hannibal, locked in the house all day, pushed him into a jog.

Opening the unlocked door he heard, with relief, Hannibal's slightly shrill puppy bark.

"It's okay, Hannibal." He dropped to his haunches to receive ecstatic, wet kisses. "It's okay." But nothing was okay. He was on the borderline of clearing his name—but unless he engineered Maglione's murder, he wouldn't be alive.

Flipping on a living room lamp, he spied the note on yellow, legal-sized paper that had been Scotch-taped to the fireplace.

I was passing and heard Hannibal carrying on. I figured you were off the island, and he needed to go out. I took him out in the back and then for a run on the beach. I left the light on in the kitchen in case you don't get back until late. Anne.

He read the note twice, folded it neatly, and put it on the mantel. He could feel Anne's presence in the house. He shed his clothes, letting them fall to the floor, and headed for the bathroom.

He remembered the light scent Anne wore. Her appealing slimness. He liked the way she looked, the way she thought, the way she made love. He liked her concern for those South Bronx kids she worked with, even though he doubted they could ever be turned around.

He flipped on the bathroom light, slid open the glass door to the shower. He leaned forward to adjust the spray to a comfortable warmth, stepped beneath the rush of water with a sigh of pleasure. Hannibal settled himself on the bath mat. He was happy that Mark was home.

For this small parcel of time under the shower Mark felt himself out in limbo. Free for these moments of the forces that were manipulating his life. Prodded by a sudden awareness of hunger, he left the shower.

Wrapped in a towel, he trailed out to the kitchen. He opened the refrigerator to inspect its contents. He stood there, frowning with distaste at the near-empty shelves, while his mind raced off on an independent track.

How fast Anne had become important to him! Damn it, he couldn't turn his life around and begin again. Approaching Fremont had been a joke. On himself.

All right. Cut the crap. Cut Annie out of his life. There was one sure way to do that. Go to her and tell her the truth. Tell her he was the ex-con who served time for allegedly raping her stepmother.

He dressed with haste. His heart hammered against his

ribs because he was cutting the fine thread that bound him to Anne. The years in stir had taught him to be a realist. Let her know who he was. Let him know the game was over.

On Wednesday at eleven he would go to Brooks's house and collect his down payment. On Saturday afternoon the hit would be made. Two weeks later he and Chuck would move on to Chicago. To their next contract. That was reality.

Hannibal barked unhappily as he prepared to leave again. Mark hesitated.

"Okay. Come on, Hannibal."

Walk over to the pizza place, he told himself. Buy a pizza and go with it to Anne's house. He ought to take her out to dinner, but he didn't want to sit across the table from her surrounded by strangers. He couldn't sit in a restaurant and tell her the truth about himself.

He zipped up his windbreaker against the night chill and walked away from the house. How different things were working out from the way he had imagined in stir.

Chuck was screwing every night. Eight times one night, he'd boasted. All *he* wanted was to make love to Annie every night in the week. She was hungry the way he was hungry.

But after tonight it would be over. He'd go to the New York apartment and play the field. He'd never even been in a singles bar. They sounded grim. Still, with the kind of money he'd be flashing, he could be choosy. *But he was too damn choosy.* All he could think about was being with Annie.

With Hannibal at his side Mark went to the pizza place. Leaving Hannibal to wait outside—no leash, but no way would Hannibal wander away—he went inside, ordered a pizza, rejoined Hannibal to watch the window for a signal that his pizza was ready.

His eyes scanned the nightwalkers with no interest. He was mentally gearing himself for what he had to do. He couldn't go on allowing Annie to believe the pack of lies he had fed her. He couldn't divide himself this way. The die had been cast.

"Stay, Hannibal." He saw the pizza being slid into a large, white box. "Stay," he repeated firmly. Somebody had taught Hannibal this basic command.

Mark headed with Hannibal for Anne's house. He was aware of the star-splashed sky. The music of the waves hitting the beach. As they approached Doris's house, a Wagnerian opera filled the air.

At Anne's house next door, lights were on in the living room and in her bedroom. But Mark was sure she was alone. She was avoiding socializing out here. That kid floundering in the water was the miracle that had brought them together. How could he not believe in fate the way this summer developed? But what did fate have in store for them in the future?

With Hannibal at his heels he mounted the stairs and crossed the deck to ring the bell. In moments Anne was pulling the door wide. She was barefoot, in jeans and a sweater, her face devoid of makeup. She looked about twelve. How could he tell her? Somewhere he must find the strength.

"In the mood for pizza?" he asked with contrived casualness.

"I'm always in the mood for pizza," she laughed.

"I brought Hannibal. He was complaining about my walking out on him. Thanks for the baby-sitting."

Anne's smile was brilliant. "Does Hannibal like pizza?"

"We'll find out." Mark handed over the box. He was in a cold sweat. He wanted to pull Annie into his arms. He wanted to carry her into the bedroom and forget everything except what it was like to be with her. Christ, he was acting like a sixteen-year-old who had just discovered sex.

"It's cool. I started a fire." He knew she sensed he was uptight. She was a barometer that read his every emotion. "It's not doing too well, though."

"I'll get it going." Mark dropped to his haunches before the fireplace. Hannibal collapsed on the hearth.

"You offering us roast dog?" he asked, smacking Hannibal affectionately on the rump. "We've got pizza coming up."

Anne brought in the pizza, transferred to an oversized tray. A bottle of Chianti was tucked under her arm. Mark reached for the tray. He held up a warning hand to Hannibal, who appeared intrigued.

"I'll get the glasses," Anne said.

In moments she was back. They sat on the floor before the fire to eat pizza and drink Chianti. The radio provided muted background music. A medley of Cole Porter tunes. Anne talked animatedly about a summer at camp. He knew she was dying to say, "Mark, what's bugging you?" But she was too sensitive to do that.

It was torture to sit here with Anne and know it was for the last time. This wasn't the way he had figured, those years of lying in a stinking cell. Life was supposed to be a merry-go-round of great times now.

Chuck would be in one of those dives of his, sizing up the women. Maybe he was already in the sack. But Mark Forrest—who used to be Mark Cameron—wanted a hell of a lot more than to get laid. He wanted a woman of his own, who belonged to every mood. He could talk to Annie. He *had* to talk to Annie, he warned himself. He couldn't walk out without explaining why.

He waited for her to clear away the remains of the pizza. Not Hannibal's cup of tea. He propped himself against a club chair and sipped Chianti until she returned.

"Annie, I have to talk to you," he said abruptly.

"All right." She dropped to the floor, sat cross-legged with an air of uneasy expectancy.

She couldn't possibly know what he was about to tell her. She wasn't prepared for this.

"Annie—" His voice sounded strange to him, but she didn't seem to notice. "I've been lying to you. All that shit about my being on the farm for six years. I was in prison. On a bum rap." He had not meant to be defensive. He was just going to lay it on the line. But the instant sympathy and support he saw in her eyes threw him off balance.

"How awful for you, Mark!" Her hand reached out for his. "But the justice system isn't perfect. Who says juries don't make mistakes?"

"I was in prison on a charge of rape!" he burst out with angry intensity. "I got a twelve to eighteen sentence. But after six years I was released for good behavior."

"You couldn't have been guilty, Mark." The compassion in her voice sent shivers through him. "I know you."

"Not guilty," he agreed with tight control. "But tried and convicted. Annie, I was the kid picked out of a line-up by Lila Schrieber. I was convicted of raping your stepmother."

"Oh, my God!" Anne was at first shocked, then enraged. "Doris was right! Lila lied." She spoke with compulsive speed in her haste to share what Doris suspected. "Mark, it must have been like what happens in this play Jeannie Walters has written about a phony charge of rape on Fire Island. The woman was having an affair. She didn't expect her husband back that evening. It was Thursday—he always came on Friday evening. She pretended to be raped to cover up for her lover, who was scrambling out the window."

"This playwright knew Lila?" Mark's throat was tight with excitement. "Annie, how much does she know about what happened that night?"

"Nothing that could be used as evidence in a court," Anne admitted. "She knew Lila from island parties. She just took the situation and built it into the play. She'd kept all the clippings on the trial, Doris said—"

"She knew the kind of woman Lila was. Annie, that's the way it must have happened!" He had never been more convinced of anything in his life.

"Lila didn't expect the case ever to reach the trial stage. She wanted to withdraw the charge. Dad wouldn't let her. He believed her."

"But she let me go to trial and be convicted." Mark's face was taut with pain. "She only cared about herself. To hell with me." Maybe she'd enjoyed punishing him for brushing off her pitch that day on the beach.

"We'll fight to clear your name," Anne said urgently. "Doris will go with you to the district attorney. I'll tell him what I know about Lila and the other men in her life."

"That's not enough—" Mark forced himself to face the truth. "Not at this point."

"What do we need?" Anne's eyes clung to his.

"We'd have to track down the man Lila was having the affair with that summer. The man who was with her that night."

Why am I talking this way? What good would it do now to clear my name? Even before talking to Fremont, I knew it was too late.

Anne rose to her feet, exuding determination. "Let's go over to Doris's house. Sit down and talk with her about this." She hesitated. "Mark, you won't mind leveling with Doris? She would never believe you could have been guilty. Not even knowing you, she suspected Lila had framed somebody."

"Okay, let's go over." Why? They were acting as though he could roll back the years and start all over again. He had a deal with Brooks. But Annie didn't know that.

"Mark—" For a moment Anne rested her body against

his. Her face brushed his. "I knew you were troubled. How awful that Lila did that to you." And then, as his arms were about to close in, she pulled away. "Let's go barge in on Doris. She's sharp. She may have some idea about how we can track down the man Lila was seeing that summer. Mark, you could go back to school. You could take the bar exams."

Her eyes shone with a warmth that twisted a knife in his gut. Annie knew about the bum rap. She didn't know about his contract with Brooks.

Anne went for sneakers and a poncho. They left Hannibal asleep by the fireplace, lamps lit about the room, and hurried from the house. At Doris's house Mark knocked on the door. Loudly, because Doris was listening to *Aida* now.

"Who is it?" Doris asked behind the door.

"Anne and Mark," Anne responded reassuringly.

The door swung wide. Doris stood there in a flattering paisley print hostess gown.

"How lovely to see you two! Come on in. What would you like to drink?"

"Nothing, thanks." Mark's smile was apologetic. "We've been guzzling Chianti all evening." It was an extravagant statement, but he wanted to sit down and talk to Doris without preliminary chitchat.

"Let me turn off the CD player." Doris walked across the living room. "Make yourselves comfortable."

"Doris, we must talk with you about something terribly important," Anne began when Doris had turned off the music and sat down. "Remember what you said about Jeannie Walters's play? And how you suspected Lila might have been lying about being raped?"

"You've found out something!" Doris's voice was electric.

"Yes—"

"I knew Lila was lying!"

"Doris, it was Mark she claimed had raped her. Mark who went to prison for six years for that."

"Oh, my God!" Doris stared from Anne to Mark with pained compassion. "And Lila let you rot in prison."

"Lila never cared about anybody but herself," Anne lashed out. "Mark had no alibi for the time she was supposed to have been raped. He was alone on the beach. She'd seen him around—she even told the police about a scar on his wrist before he was brought in."

"Lila took a chance," Doris said. "He could have had an alibi."

"She was gambling that he didn't. She could always say she was upset and made a mistake. But right away it came out that Mark had no alibi. And Lila sat there in that courtroom every day of the trial, knowing what she was doing to him." Anne trembled in rage.

"What must we do to clear you, Mark?" Doris asked. "God knows, we can't repay you for those years in prison. At least, let's try to straighten out the records."

"The only way to get through to the DA is if we can come up with the man who was with Lila that specific Thursday night," Mark said. He ignored the mocking voice in his mind that said, *What the hell are you doing?* "You wouldn't know his name?"

"No. But I've seen him on the island this summer. Twice," Doris recalled, and Mark felt a surge of excitement. "He was out a few times last summer, too. He'd stayed away the earlier summers. I always noticed because something bothered me about the whole scene." She squinted in recall. "He has a coarse sexuality. I guess that turned on Lila. He looked about twenty-eight then, but he's not wearing well," she said with a caustic smile. "Plenty of money, expensive

suits, Gucci shoes—but he talks too loud and has an arrogant
air. Probably clawed his way out of the slums. He didn't pick
up any polish—"

"Doris, where did you see him?" Mark broke in. "On the
beach?"

"On the beach one morning about two weeks ago. Once in
the seafood restaurant. He wears a wedding band, but you
can be sure the woman he was with wasn't his wife."

"If you saw him on the beach," Mark turned to Lila, "and
we could get a snapshot of him—"

"We could show it around at the restaurants," Anne
picked up. "Maybe somebody would know his name."

"We can try that," Mark conceded, "but I doubt we'll
come up with a name. If he's out here with a woman not his
wife, he isn't handing out his business cards."

"What will you do if you find him?" Anne pursued. "He's
not going to admit he was with Lila that night."

Mark's smile was a blend of conviction and cynicism. "I
learned a few things in prison. He'll admit it."

"Why would he admit it?" Doris challenged. "Wouldn't
he be criminally involved?"

"A sharp lawyer will get him clear if I don't press," Mark
said quietly. "If we could locate the guy, we'd scare the hell
out of him. He'd be an accessory to a false arrest and conviction. We push him to go to the district attorney with some
cooked-up story. He'd been out of the country—he didn't
know what was happening." *So what good will that do now? I
have a commitment to Brooks. My butt is on the line.*

Despite the coolness of the evening, Mark broke out in a
sweat. No matter where he went from here, he was driven by a
compulsion to clear himself of that rape conviction.

"You point him out, Doris," Mark said. "Let me take it
from there."

Chapter Twenty-One

Though he and Anne had sat on her deck gazing out at the night ocean until close to dawn, Mark awoke early that morning. He awoke with an instant awareness of the day's schedule. A blend of tension and anticipation welled in him.

At ten he would pick up Doris. They would spend the morning on the beach inspecting faces. If Doris was right, the creep would be on the island today, go back sometime tomorrow. If they were lucky and spotted Lila's lover, he would tail the guy, find out where he was staying. After that he'd have to play it by ear.

At the foot of the bed Hannibal lifted his head. Eager for horseplay.

"Okay, Hannibal." He leaned forward to wrestle for a few moments while his mind focused on the morning's search. Now he pushed aside the light blanket and crossed the room to pull swimming trunks from a drawer. He'd run down to the beach for a quick swim. Plenty of time for that.

He stifled a yawn. He had not stayed over at Annie's last night—though he'd wanted to do that—because he hadn't trusted himself to get up in time this morning. She'd been disappointed, he suspected.

"Come on, Hannibal. Breakfast." He'd have a fast breakfast, go down to the beach for a swim. Nobody would be out this early.

In twenty minutes Mark was on the beach. Another glorious morning—the sun dazzling even at this early hour. Not a cloud in the sky. But it would be another scorcher. The sand was already warm under his feet.

As he'd guessed, only a pair of joggers were down this early. Nobody in the water. Hannibal barked vociferously at the waves, seemed to be fighting an urge to jump in.

"Hannibal, it's great," Mark tempted, striding out into the water. God, how often he had visualized this in stir! Sometimes, lying in his bunk, he could almost taste the salt spray in his mouth.

He swam out until caution ordered him closer to shore. He knew that Hannibal was splashing in and out at the water's edge in obvious delight. All right, enough, he told himself. Playtime was over.

"Come on, Hannibal," he called, out of the water now. "Let's go home."

Walking up from the beach, he gazed involuntarily towards Anne's house. Her bedroom drapes were drawn tight. She would sleep late this morning. How rotten, to be handed a slice of heaven and know it would soon be taken away from him.

He returned to the house with Hannibal, showered and dressed, then staked himself out on a chaise on the deck. Early yet, he told himself. He wasn't to pick up Doris until 10:00 a.m. But his mind was a traitor and zeroed in on what taunted him. There was no way—*no way*—that he could hand back that contract to Brooks. Not if he wanted to stay alive.

In prison—with frustration eating away at him, knowing he was innocent—he'd clung to his plan to utilize the law to his advantage as a means of survival. It gave him a reason for staying alive. For keeping out of trouble. Meeting Annie had turned him around. The possibility of clearing himself, of going to law school, tore at his gut.

Why couldn't he have waited a month before jumping into the business with those punks? Why did he have to jump in when the taste of prison was still rancid in his mouth? He had to show himself how smart he was. He had to come out of that pigsty ahead of the game.

Without him, Chuck would have gone right back on the street—pushing hard drugs again. Chuck was an older version of those kids Annie was so upset about. Like them, Chuck could kill and feel no remorse.

Restless, Mark abandoned the chaise to go inside. He'd walk to the village, buy the *New York Times*. Kill some time until he was to pick up Doris.

He was impatient to be walking along the beach with her. Watching for a glint of recognition in her eyes. It could happen. Crazier things happened.

Walking to the newspaper store, he inspected every male face in view, Doris's description etched across his brain. A man emerging from the luncheonette stopped him dead. All at once his breathing was labored. This guy fit Doris's description right down to the Adidas sneakers.

Mark's eyes focused on the large browned left hand. A wedding band shone in the sunlight. A moment later a pair of youngsters crashed forward yelling, "Hey, Daddy!" and a young woman in shorts and T-shirt came towards him with a grocery bag. No, this wasn't Lila's lover. It wasn't going to be that easy.

At ten sharp he was at Doris's door. A beach robe over her swimsuit, dark glasses in hand, she came forward with a brilliant smile.

"Let's go down to the beach," he said with a false air of confidence. "We've got to find a man."

The beach was sparsely littered with bodies. Not until the weekend would there be any real competition for space on the sand. Mark and Doris walked slowly, ostensibly in casual conversation. Mark felt a tightness in his throat as he waited for Doris to spot their quarry. They covered the length of beach, turned around and retraced their steps. Doris was taking this search with grim seriousness.

"He's not on the beach this morning," she admitted at last. "Let's go check out the stores."

There were few people in the shops this early. In the grocery store Doris shopped, all the while keeping an eye on the entrance. Now she and Mark headed for the cashier.

"Let me take your bag—" Mark reached to take it from her when she'd paid the cashier.

Now Doris stopped to chat with a pair of women acquaintances. She introduced Mark as a neighbor without any amplifications. He saw the glow of curiosity in their eyes. Not because he looked familiar, he was sure. They were wondering if Doris was having herself a fling with the younger generation.

"Let's go to Anne's and keep a lookout from her deck for a while," Doris decided. "If he's out here today, we'll find him."

Mark and Doris headed home. They allowed no face to go unnoticed as they walked. At her house Doris paused and took the bundle of groceries Mark carried for her.

"I'll put this away and join you at Annie's," she said with a sympathetic smile. "Don't look so grim. I'm getting vibes that tell me we're going to nail that creep."

"Sure." Mark forced a smile.

"Tell Annie I'll fix one of my fancy salads for the three of us later. Don't make plans for lunch."

Mark approached the house. The open door told him Anne was awake. He walked inside, called, "Annie?"

"In the kitchen." The lilt in her voice was a reassuring welcome.

"No luck," he announced and reached to pull her to him.

"First morning?" she reproached. "Nobody's that lucky."

He kissed her urgently—welcoming her response—then released her.

"Doris'll be right here. We're setting up a watch on your deck," he said with an effort at humor. "And Doris has invited us for lunch."

They settled themselves on chaises on the deck with coffee mugs in tow. Minutes later Doris arrived. She positioned herself in a chair facing the beach. Without losing sight of any new arrival, she talked effervescently about her last summer tour, fraught with humorous mishaps.

Fighting a surge of frustration, Mark left his chaise to stand by the railing. How could they be sure Lila's lover would ever show? He ought to hire a private investigator. Let somebody with professional know-how dig into this. Maybe that guy whose card he'd been carrying for two years. The inmate who'd given it to him said this guy was supposed sharp and inexpensive—as PIs went.

"I'm going home to make my absolutely irresistible salad," Doris said after a while. "You two come over in about forty-five minutes. After a long lunch we'll go barhopping. Out here that won't be extensive," Doris reminded, "but it might be profitable."

"Mark, relax," Anne urged gently when they were alone.

Mark swung about to face her. Knowing there was only one way he could wash away the tension that tied him in knots.

"Annie, let's go inside."

"All right." Her face luminous, she rose to her feet and extended a hand to him.

★ ★ ★ ★ ★

After they had made love, they lay tangled together in the darkened room—reluctant to break the spell that engulfed them. Knowing there was a little time yet before they must show at Doris's house. Each time he made love to Annie, he was making it worse for her, Mark tormented himself. She knew about the phony rape charge. She didn't know about Brooks. *How am I to tell her?*

"It's funny the things you remember," Anne mused, her head on his shoulder. "When I was a little girl, I felt so awful because I didn't have a mother. Other kids had parents who were separated or divorced—but I didn't *have* a mother. But Dad was wonderful—he tried to be both dad and mother to me."

"What kind of schools did you go to?" he asked. "Private, I'll bet." In his suburban world good public schools had been sufficient.

"I went to private schools because Dad was so determined to give me the best. But I looked around, and I saw half the kids were going to psychologists or psychiatrists. We had a neighbor—a divorced woman lawyer—whose four-year-old was seeing a shrink twice a week. In our small school they had four guidance counselors. Somebody was always with each one. Crying or being rebellious. I was rebellious for a while— right after Dad married Lila." Her smile was wry. "But I got a handle on that."

"All adolescents are rebellious," Mark scoffed. "Only some get carried away."

"I didn't resent Lila," Anne said with honesty. "I hated her because right away I knew what she was. That was the year I decided I absolutely hated school. Lila slept till noon every day—she never knew what was going on with me. I'd meet my friend Candy, and we'd wander around Manhattan."

"Washington Square Park, the East Village," he guessed. "I remember a period when a couple of buddies and I made that trek on weekends."

"Candy and I both lived in the East Seventies. The clean, beautiful East Seventies. Then one day we walked north about thirty blocks. East Harlem was a brutal shock. I think that was the day I decided to become a social worker."

"I liked to come into Manhattan and walk around the Columbia campus. I'd read those books about the Columbia rebellion and was fascinated."

"Candy picked up a Puerto Rican guitar player and got pregnant by him. He was a sweet, earnest kid. He wanted to get married, quit school, and join some rock group. Candy had an abortion in some fancy private sanitarium in the Caribbean and came back to school unpregnant and gorgeously tanned. She never saw her guitar player again."

"We'd better go to Doris's place," Mark said reluctantly. "If that salad wilts, she'll refuse to be a witness for me."

The three of them dawdled over lunch, served on the deck—where they could watch for their quarry. Mark was conscious of soaring tension. Was that bastard on the island? Were they just spinning their wheels?

"Okay, kids, let's try the bars," Doris said briskly when they'd finished their lunch. "I've got a pretty good idea he spends more time on a bar stool than on the beach. Mark, go dress."

Nobody would suspect their objective, Mark thought with bitter humor as he strolled with Anne and Doris in the direction of Doris's favorite bar. Yet underneath their convivial conversation, Mark felt the sense of urgency that churned within each of them.

They lingered at the bar until Doris indicated they should try another. This was not going to work, Mark warned himself as they took their leave. He'd have to contact that PI he learned about in stir. Because he knew that whatever happened, he wanted to be cleared of raping Lila Schrieber.

They nursed one drink at the second bar until Doris announced she must go home to dress for a dinner date.

"It's somebody I can't afford to put off," she apologized. "It's a man who's putting up most of the money for Jeannie Walters's play. I met him at her party."

"I defrosted a steak," Anne said. "Mark and I will have a cookout on the deck."

"You brought steaks out in an insulated bag," Mark guessed, suddenly nostalgic.

"Yes," Anne said softly. "Dad used to do that on weekends."

"Doesn't everybody?" Doris joshed. "Mark, pick me up tomorrow morning at ten a.m. again. Nobody's going to be on the beach before then."

"I have to go to Bay Shore first thing in the morning," he said uncomfortably and paused, aware that Doris expected fuller information. "I ought to be back early in the afternoon," he added awkwardly.

"Good. Anne and I will do the beach and lunch search," Doris decided. "When you return, we'll try the beach again. Then we'll go to my seafood place for dinner. The creep seemed to like that. Don't blame him—it's great." Doris nodded in approval. "We'll go early, stay late. Annie, I'll pick you up tomorrow morning around ten—okay?"

"Fine." Anne nodded. But Mark saw the questions in her eyes. What was so important that he'd abandon this urgent search for several hours to go to Bay Shore?

Mark and Anne stopped at his house to pick up Hannibal, were greeted with the usual ecstatic welcome. Then they made a stop at Anne's house so she could change into slacks and a light sweater. Now they headed for the beach to give Hannibal a run before dinner. Like Anne, Mark was beginning to appreciate this time of day on the beach—when it was all but deserted.

"It would have been useless for us to go out to dinner without Doris," Anne said somberly while they strolled over the sand and Hannibal raced up and down at the water's edge. "Only she can identify him."

"I prefer dinner on the deck—alone with you," he said in quiet satisfaction.

"I'll like that, too."

"Maybe we'll be lucky at dinner tomorrow. At the seafood place where Doris saw him twice." *This whole deal is crazy. I find him—so what? That won't change things for Annie and me.*

They gave Hannibal a lengthy run and returned to Anne's house. Mark brought out the hibachi, prepared the charcoal for the steaks. Inside the house Anne was preparing fresh corn and a salad. She was singing with the radio. Slightly off-key, which somehow seemed endearing to Mark.

They ate on the deck—facing a solitary beach, a deserted ocean. The setting sun was like a massive museum masterpiece hanging in the distance, Mark thought—knowing he would forever remember tonight with Anne. It was as though he was storing up every precious moment with her to sustain him in the empty years ahead.

What he had forced himself to regard as a triumphant future mocked him with its ugliness. But he was committed. There was no turning back.

Chapter Twenty-Two

Mark leaned across Anne to shut off the alarm before it could wake her. He had set the alarm to make sure he didn't oversleep. As he set the alarm last night, Anne had watched him with wistful anxiety. She'd hoped he would tell her where he was going. *How could I tell her?*

He left the bed and dressed. He'd have to run home, shave, shower, change clothes. He paused for a moment at the side of the bed to gaze down at Anne, sprawled in slumber. So lovely. So vulnerable.

Hannibal was dozing in a swathe of sunlight that poured in through the glass expanse in the living room. The moment Mark walked into the room he was awake.

"Come on, boy."

Talk to Hannibal. Don't think about what was happening at ten this morning. Christ, he ought to be riding high! At ten o'clock he would carry off one hundred twenty-five thousand tax-free dollars. Why did he feel as though he was moving into death row? But he knew why.

Back at his own house Mark shaved, showered, dressed, prepared himself a cup of instant coffee. He drank it while Hannibal, with his voracious puppy appetite, put away a heavy breakfast.

Mark kept his eyes on his watch. He couldn't afford to miss the ferry this morning. Chuck would pick him up on the

155

other side, go with him to Brooks, and then they'd take the money to the bank. He'd told Chuck to leave the punks at a diner a few miles down the road. Chuck could pick them up later and head for the dump.

Chuck said this was a fancy game to them, with the payoff like the jackpot on a TV game show. It didn't mean a damn to them that they were going to kill a guy. Sociopaths—the kind that Annie hoped to change into human beings.

A coldness closed in around Mark. Those kids were preparing—training—to kill at his orders. He tried to dismiss this. What the hell was the matter with him? He was a realist, and he was taking the only road open to him.

He left the house. Hannibal complained indignantly behind the closed door. But Anne would look in on him later. Probably take him for a run on the beach.

Mark strode towards the dock. He was conscious of a pleasing coolness this morning, which was welcome after the record heat wave of the past few days.

Everything must move on schedule today. He had worked long and hard on this project. How did he know he'd ever find Lila's lover and clear himself? The chances were minuscule. This deal with Brooks was real—plus he had to pull it off if he was to stay alive.

Anne awoke with an instant awareness that she was alone in bed. Subconsciously she reached out one hand to caress the area where Mark had lain during the night. Where had he gone today? Was there another woman in his life? Someone who had waited for him to get out of prison?

Disturbed by such truant thoughts, Anne left the bed and went in to shower. She'd have to do some shopping at the grocery store this morning. She didn't expect any mail, but from habit she'd stop at the post office. After that she'd go over to

Mark's house and let Hannibal have a run. The key would be in the usual place.

When she had shopped, subconsciously inspecting every male face in the stores, Anne went over to the post office. She'd received a postcard from Claire, on a gambling spree in Atlantic City. Curiously she gazed at a tube addressed to her. It looked as thought it might contain a calendar, though this was hardly the time of year to receive a calendar.

The tube was heavily marked "First Class" and stamped "Special Handling." Then she read the scrawled return address. It was from Joey Devlin.

Juggling parcels and the mailing tube she went to Mark's house. Hannibal was scratching at the door as she approached. She went inside, made love to him, then let him out the back for a run. Now she stored her parcels in Mark's refrigerator until she was ready to return to her own house.

At the kitchen table she carefully pulled out the contents of the tube, spread the paper flat across the table. It was a vibrant watercolor by Joey, signed in the right-hand corner as she had taught him to do in an effort to raise his self-esteem.

She inspected the watercolor with pleasure. The figures were crude, primitive, and exciting—but the feeling was intense. Joey was painting the world he knew with a power that was impressive.

She must show this work to Mark, she told herself. Chris and Mark were so sure that sociopaths could not be turned around. But this watercolor had not been executed by a sociopath.

According to schedule, Mark found Chuck waiting for him on the mainland.

"I dumped the kids in the diner like you said," Chuck reported as Mark slid beside him on the front seat of the car.

157

"We got plenty of time to make it to Brooks's house." His eyes glittered. Mentally he was already spending his share of the take.

"We're early. Let's go somewhere for coffee."

They lingered briefly over coffee, then headed for Brooks's estate. Again they were met at the gates by a hood with a bulging hip. This morning they were sent directly up to the house.

Chuck parked in the circular driveway. Mark and he walked up the entrance to the house. As though waiting for their arrival, the maid opened the door and without a word led them to Brooks's office.

Brooks sat behind his desk in the overly air-conditioned room. His eyes were cold. Penetrating. The same pair of tall burly hoods flanked him. Mark noted the cheap plastic attaché case that sat at one corner of the desk.

"Good morning," Mark said—as diffidently as he might have greeted a respected client if he were a practicing attorney.

"You're prepared?" Brooks was brusque.

"We'll carry out the hit as arranged." He felt like an actor in a bad TV melodrama. "All the details have been worked out. Saturday afternoon as Maglione goes in to the wedding reception. We'll have a dry run on Friday." Brooks had not invited him to sit down, but the attaché case was mute testimony that they were here to consummate the financial arrangements.

"No mistakes, Forrest," Brooks warned. "I don't tolerate mistakes."

"I'm not in business to make mistakes," Mark said tersely.

"I want it understood," Brooks emphasized. "You're new in the field. We've got no time for slip-ups. I get upset. Do the job, and we'll have other business. Sit down." Now he waved a hand towards a chair. It was obvious he meant for Chuck to remain standing.

Mark sat down with a surface casualness. The money designated for him was there in that attaché case. Brooks wouldn't be caught in a back alley with junk like that.

"Give me an address and phone number where you can be reached if Maglione changes his plans. I've got somebody close to him to keep me up to the minute," Brooks told him.

"Contact Chuck," Mark said warily.

"I don't want to contact your man. I want to contact you." Suddenly Brooks's eyes were menacing. "I don't deal with the hired help."

"I don't have a telephone where I'm staying for the summer," Mark explained. "It's wiser in my business." He allowed himself an arrogant smile. "I'm staying at my family's house on Fire Island."

"Okay, give me the address." Brooks relaxed. "I've got a cabin cruiser. If I need to reach you, I'll send somebody out."

"Sure." Mark gave him the location of the house, with directions from the dock.

"Here." Brooks picked up a key from his desk, tossed it to Mark. "Count it." He pointed towards the attaché case. "Just so we agree there's no mistake. And it stays in the bank until after the hit."

Aware of the hostility of the two hoods—who obviously distrusted this operation—Mark unlocked the case. The room was heavy with silence as he lifted the lid. He heard Chuck's involuntary intake of breath. One hundred twenty-five thousand dollars lay stacked in neat rows of fifties and hundreds. Methodically Mark flipped through each sheaf of bills, checking denominations rather than counting.

"It's here." Mark snapped the lid shut, locked the case. He dropped the key in his jacket pocket, lifted the case from the desk. "We'll collect the balance after the hit. Immediately after," he emphasized.

With a polite nod to Brooks, ignoring the hoods, Mark walked from the room with Chuck beside him. They continued in silence down the corridor, out of the house and to the car. Chuck drove down the driveway and out through the gates, opened at their approach by the man on duty.

"Holy shit!" Chuck's voice rippled with excitement. "I never seen so much loot in one place in my life! Like we was on a TV show!" He glanced slyly at Mark. "Hey, Attorney, how about advancin' me a grand?"

"We don't touch it until we've made the hit," Mark reminded.

"Aw, Mark, a stinkin' grand? Come on, let's live a little."

"No," Mark brushed this aside. "We don't touch the payoff until we've collected in full."

"Yeah, I know that's what you told the kids. But between us?" Chuck wheedled. "There's this chick—"

"Chuck, forget it."

He saw the rage soar in Chuck. He knew Chuck was capable of hitting him over the head and taking off with the attaché case. But he had saved Chuck's life that time in the slammer. That was his insurance.

"Okay," Chuck capitulated. Yet instinct warned Mark to keep a tight rein on Chuck. "Where to now?"

Mark gave him directions to the bank. In twenty minutes Chuck pulled up before a low red-brick building with white shutters and a porte cochere that featured a drive-in window for those wishing to conduct their banking without leaving the car.

"This is it?" Chuck was skeptical. "It don't look like no bank to me."

"It's a bank." Mark reached for the attaché case. His mind

was shaping his next moves. Chuck must see the money go into the box. All of a sudden the Chuck he had known in prison had been replaced by the street Chuck who trusted no one. "Come inside."

"That case is a piece of shit," Chuck said with contempt. "I'll bet Brooks had one of his guys pick it up at a drugstore for ten bucks."

"Did you expect something from Vuitton?" Mark asked with a chuckle.

"Who's he? Some fancy fence?"

Inside the bank Mark and Chuck went downstairs. Chuck was uncomfortable in the casualness of the suburban bank.

"You'll have to wait for me here," Mark explained as they approached the barred partition. "I give the man there my key. He takes the bank key. With both keys he opens up the box. You can see it all from here. I'll make the transfer into the box and come right out."

The man on duty remembered him from the day he had arranged for the switch to the larger box. He greeted him cordially. Mark was conscious of Chuck's eyes as he waited for the box to be brought from the inner vault. Chuck's eyes followed him as the attendant carried the box to one of the cubicles and deposited it on the table inside.

"Take your time, sir," the attendant said genially and closed the door behind Mark.

Mark made the transfer from attaché case to box. In prison he had anticipated this action with such relish. It was partial payment for what the government had taken away from him. He brought out the box, empty attaché case in his free hand, and exchanged pleasantries with the attendant. Now he rejoined Chuck on the other side of the barred divider.

"Okay," Mark said. "Drive me back to the ferry. Then pick up the kids. Everything going okay with them?"

"Sure. Like a picnic." Chuck grinned. "How could they miss a target eight to ten feet away?"

"We'll have the dry run on Friday," Mark reminded. "You don't come out here. I'll come into New York and meet you at the pool hall. Clear?"

"Clear."

In the car Mark deliberately opened the attaché case to assure Chuck it was empty. He dropped the key inside, shut it, and tossed the case to the rear seat.

"Jesus, we'd better get movin'. Them three in the diner will be scared I blew town." Chuck slid the key into the ignition. His eyes were opaque. He was still sore at not getting that grand advance, Mark interpreted.

Chuck couldn't wait to get his hands on his share of the take because it was going to make him a big man on the street—until he blew it. But there would be more in a few weeks, Mark reminded himself brutally. This wasn't a one-shot operation. Three more to go, then they'd close up shop—before the fuzz saw the pattern.

He hadn't wanted Brooks to know where he was staying, he thought in simmering annoyance. Why did the bastard have to corner him that way? It had been a bad mistake to go out to Fire Island. If he had not met Annie—if he had not found out about Lila's lover—he could have gone through this scene without sweating this way.

Chapter Twenty-Three

Anne sat on the deck with an opened copy of *Newsweek* across her knees and a mug of coffee on the table to her left. She and Doris had walked on the beach for almost two hours, had lunch at a popular restaurant. No sign of Lila's lover. Had he skipped coming out this week?

Doris was taking a nap now—preparing herself for what she called the afternoon and dinnertime shift. But Doris was as anxious as she, Anne told herself, to find Lila's lover. Was Mark right? Could he convince the creep to go to the district attorney, admit what actually happened?

In a gesture of frustration, Anne tossed the magazine onto the table. She couldn't read. She was trying to convince herself she wasn't disturbed by Mark's running off to Bay Shore this morning with no explanation.

Go over to Mark's place. Let Hannibal out in the back for a while again. Mark left early. It was past one already. What was so important that he had to go to Bay Shore this morning?

Hannibal gave her a noisy welcome. He charged towards the nearest bush when she held the kitchen door wide for him to go out. She crossed to the backyard chaise, lowered herself into it. Moments later Hannibal came to sit beside her.

Fondling Hannibal, she worried about Mark. He was

fighting some horrific inner battle. But she mustn't pry. That would drive him more deeply into himself.

If they could clear Mark, he'd feel he could lead a normal life again. Last night he said something vague about a private investigator. Did he have enough money to handle a situation like that? She'd help if he'd let her.

"Hannibal, come back here!" she called as he darted after a cat. "Hannibal!"

She waited forty minutes for Mark to appear. When he didn't show, she took Hannibal inside, gave him a bowl of fresh water, and left.

It was almost three o'clock when Mark hurried from the ferry to the house. He was exhausted. Stress, he told himself. Had Annie and Doris found their guy? He'd stretch out for a quick nap, then check with them.

Hannibal greeted him as though they'd been separated for days. He was sure Annie had come over and given him a run—but when he opened the door Hannibal chased outside.

God, he was living a schizoid existence! Chasing after Lila's lover to clear his name while he operated a twelve-year-old hit factory. But clearing himself had become an obsession.

For the rest of today, forget about the contract, he exhorted himself. Focus on finding Lila's lover. All the guy had to do was to admit that he was with Lila just before her husband came into the house. Let Doris identify him—then he'd scare the shit out of him. He'd make the bastard go to the DA.

If nothing happened tonight, he promised himself, he'd put a call through to that PI in Manhattan. Doris was into this thing all the way. She'd give the PI all the help she could.

With Hannibal back in the house, he stretched out on the sofa. In minutes he was sound asleep. He woke up with a start almost two hours later. Damn, Anne and Doris must be full of questions. If they found the guy, he was supposed to tail him.

How did he explain his absence all day?

All right, get off your ass, he reproached himself. Go over to Anne's—the three of them were to have dinner tonight at the seafood place. In a compulsive rush he left the house—hearing Hannibal's plaintive barks as he walked away.

Anne was on the deck. Her eyes glowed with welcome. "Hi."

"I'm sorry I couldn't get back earlier," he apologized.

"It's been a long, dull day. Nothing accomplished." Anne lifted her face to his as he bent to kiss her.

"I should have been with you—"

"Doris is the key player," she reminded. "We looked." Her eyes were suddenly troubled. "I heard from one of my kids. I hate to think of him running around loose in the sweltering city. His mother is a hooker—sleeps all day, works at night."

"Annie, stop worrying about them," Mark chided. "You know the statistics. One of five arrests for major crimes involves a kid under sixteen. They figure the law gives them a license." Anger mixed with defensiveness in him as he spoke. "All records are sealed. The cops can't even fingerprint them. When they come out of reform schools, they're not even in mug books at the Bureau of Criminal Identification."

"We don't get to them early enough," Anne protested. "Kids who commit murders showed hostile behavior at five. Studies prove that. They spring from troubled families. They were abused. Their parents were emotionally unstable. They're retarded in reading, inarticulate. Mark, it never gets better for them because they're born and bred in ignorance and poverty."

"Plenty of kids come out of the ghettos and make it," Mark shot back.

"You sound like Chris. But not every kid has that strength. We have to reach them early. We have to reach their parents. We have to improve their living conditions!"

"It was rotten living on the Lower East Side at the turn of the century," Mark retaliated, "but from there emerged judges and scientists and financiers. Not a generation of teenage murderers and rapists. The city builds low-income housing projects and they become giant privies."

"You're talking about the rotten five or ten percent." Anne leaned forward earnestly. "Like the way people talk about bad cops. So there are five or ten percent on the take. The rest are putting their lives on the line every day!"

"What about those three kids you were telling me about?" Mark pursued. "The ones that gave lifetime traumas to those two little boys. Are the courts doing them a favor showing them they can get away with anything?"

"Will it help to throw them in with adult criminals?" Anne challenged. "Mark, you know what would happen to them."

"We need more facilities," Mark agreed. "Not the turnstile reform schools or the mental hospitals where the kids can cut out with no sweat or be signed out by their parents. We need tight security facilities with in-depth, long-term psychiatric care. Not one psychiatrist to cope with three or four hundred kids. We need to remove those kids from society— early, like you said," Mark said tiredly. "But who's going to pick up the tab?"

"Mark, you have such a feel for this situation," Anne said. He winced. She didn't know how he was using this situation. "Once you're cleared, you can go to law school. As an attorney, you could be so useful in fighting for reforms."

Mark rose to his feet. "I'm dying of thirst. Have you got anything cold in the refrigerator?"

"A pitcher of iced tea and of apple juice." She rose from the chaise, and—arm in arm—they walked into the house. In the kitchen she went to the refrigerator, pulled the door wide. "Oh, there's a cold beer," she noticed and pulled out the bottle. But Mark was drawn to the watercolor newly attached to a kitchen wall.

"What's this?" he asked, drawn to the crude yet vital picture.

"That came in the mail," Anne said softly. "It was sent by one of the three kids I told you about—the one I refuse to believe is a sociopath." She pointed to the signature in the lower right-hand corner. "Twelve-year-old Joey Devlin, who lives in a nightmare."

Mark froze. Joey Devlin's ingenuous face danced before his eyes. He felt as though a hammer had smashed into his skull. Anne's school was in the South Bronx. The Joey Devlin on his team was twelve and from the South Bronx. *It had to be the same boy.*

God, what crazy tricks is fate playing with my life?

Chapter Twenty-Four

Wearing an elegant gray silk pantsuit, Doris was waiting for them when Mark and Anne arrived at her door.

"Let me get my glasses," she delayed them for a moment. "I can't read the menu without them."

With the glasses stashed in a case in her purse, Doris prodded them out the front door.

"I checked out the beach this morning. No sign of him," she said, "but Annie must have told you that. That doesn't mean he won't be at the restaurant. We'll sit there a long time. The restaurant won't be crowded on a midweek night."

They walked briskly, each conscious of what it would mean to Mark to nab Lila's lover. Would Doris be so eager to help him, Mark taunted himself, if she knew his present vocation?

The restaurant was devoid of diners except for a trio of elderly white-haired ladies dressed as though they were attending an embassy dinner. A man and two girls were in avid conversation at the bar.

Mark sat with Anne and Doris at a table with a clear view of the entrance. Doris inquired of the waiter about the condition of his daughter, recently injured in a car smash-up. Mark was tense—his eyes focused on the entrance.

"I'm having my usual problem," Anne confided. "I adore

veal, but my conscience won't allow me to eat it. Not knowing how those poor little calves are treated."

"Darling, it's sacrilegious to have anything but seafood here," Doris said. She brought out her glasses and concentrated on the menu.

The three discussed the menu with mock seriousness, debating about what to order. Anne's smile was strained, Mark noted with compunction. Like him, she would hardly know what she ate.

Diners began to filter into the room. Doris scrutinized each arrival. Nobody that fitted her description appeared. Mark joined in the table conversation, but part of his mind had flashed back to the days of his trial. He could hear Lila's voice spewing out lies about him, weaving the net that convicted him.

"Mark, you're not eating," Anne scolded.

The waiter came to clear their table. He brought menus so they could decide on desserts. Doris pulled out her glasses again.

"I shouldn't be having sweets," she said dramatically. "I must drop eighteen pounds. But I have no resistance when I know they have the most sumptuous Black Forest cake here."

All at once Mark saw Doris's hands tighten on her menu. Her eyes were fastened on a couple settling themselves at the bar. Mark's throat went dry with excitement.

"The man who just came in with the girl in the black off-the-shoulder dress," Doris whispered. "That's Lila's lover. I'd swear it in any court."

For a moment Mark was immobile. He stared at the man in expensive but flashy clothes. His mind reached out for an approach. How the hell was he to get the guy out of the bar?

"Doris, let me have the case to your glasses," Mark said under his breath. He extended his hand below table level. Silently Doris complied.

Mark pushed back his chair and rose to his feet.

Doris turned to Anne. "Darling, are you having the Black Forest cake?"

Mark walked to the bar. He stationed himself at the opposite end from the pair who had just arrived. He dug the nails of one hand into his palm in his effort to appear casual.

"Jim, my usual," the man said loudly as he hovered above the attractive young blonde. "And make it fast."

Mark waited for Jim to serve the other two. Then Jim came to stand before him.

"What are you having?" Jim asked breezily.

Mark leaned forward with an air of good-humored conspiracy.

"The guy at the end of the bar looks an awful lot like somebody I used to know. Would you happen to know his name?"

Jim's eyes were cynical.

"He calls himself Clint Jones," he said dryly. He smiled as Mark slid a bill across the counter. "If he gets over his amnesia, I'll remember till the next time you come in."

"Thanks, Jim."

Clint Jones was leaving his girl to cross to the men's room. Mark took a swift inventory of the sparsely tenanted dining room. At this hour the men's room was likely to be empty. He slid from the bar stool and followed Jones.

Lila's lover was standing at a washbasin dumping a small yellow pill into his hand. With a fleeting self-conscious glance about him he popped the pill into his mouth, turned on the cold water, and put his cupped hands beneath the flow. Mark made a pretense of washing his hands as Jones finished his pill gulping.

"Mr. Jones, I want to talk to you," Mark said with menacing calm while the other man dried his hands.

"What about?" Jones was belligerent.

"At my house." With one hand in his jacket pocket Mark moved in close. Jones's eyes were drawn to the concealed hand. "We both want this to be private."

"You can't do this to me!" Jones blustered. "I'll yell for the cops."

"You'll be dead when they arrive. And I'll be out that window behind you."

"What the hell is this all about? My doctor just gave me Valium to keep me from being so uptight. I don't need this crap."

"You want to stay alive you'll walk quietly out of this room with me and out the front door. But first tell your girlfriend I'm a business associate, and that you'll be back in fifteen minutes. No funny stuff. I'm just out of stir. I lost my sense of humor there."

"Okay, okay. Cool it." Jones moistened his lower lip with the tip of his tongue. He was uneasy about being hassled by an ex-con. "I'll tell Ginger I'll be back in ten minutes."

"Fifteen," Mark corrected. "Five minutes to walk to my place, five minutes to come back. I can say what I have to say in the other five." His eyes were calculatedly cold. The hand in his pocket moved towards Jones. "Remember, it won't bother me if I have to use this."

"Yeah, sure." Jones was sweating. "We'll talk."

Mark stayed at his side while they paused at the bar so he could tell the blonde he'd be back in fifteen minutes. She was annoyed. He tossed a bill on the counter and told Jim to bring Ginger a refill.

"All right, let's go," Mark said under his breath. "No funny business." Anne and Doris would see him leave with the guy. They'd wait at the restaurant. But he noted with astonishment that Anne wasn't at their table. Perhaps she'd gone to the powder room.

Mark and Jones walked in silence to Mark's house. He had left the door unlocked. A lamp was lit in the living room to keep Hannibal company.

"Open the door and walk inside," Mark ordered.

Instantly Hannibal began to bark. Jones froze.

"Don't worry," Mark said. "He's a friendly pup. Go on in."

Hannibal uttered a low, menacing growl that faded as he spied Mark.

"Okay, Hannibal. Lie down," he said with unfamiliar sternness, and Hannibal collapsed into a heap of fur in front of the sofa.

"What's this all about?" Jones demanded. "I don't walk around with a lotta cash."

"I don't want your money," Mark told him with contempt. "Let me see your wallet."

Jones reached into his pocket and pulled out his wallet. He handed it to Mark. He was anxious, uncertain about Mark's next move.

With his left hand Mark flipped open the wallet. He saw the driver's license. The car registration. Clinton Rossiter. A Vermont address. He probably owned a Vermont vacation house and used the address to save on car insurance and license plates.

"Catch." Mark threw the wallet back to him. "My name is Mark Cameron." He watched for a flicker of recognition in Rossiter's eyes. "The jerk who got framed for raping Lila Schrieber."

"I don't know anything about that," Rossiter shot back, but he was getting the message.

"You know everything about it. You were the guy in the sack with her when I was supposed to be raping her. Her husband came home a day early. You took a dive out the window."

"That's bullshit!" Rossiter's face was flushed.

"Lila picked me out of the line-up and nailed me with a rape charge. You were screwing her when her husband arrived. That's why the doctor found semen when he examined her."

"I never knew her!" Rossiter's voice was strident. "You don't know what you're talking about!"

"I've got witnesses who'll swear you were having an affair with Lila that summer. They knew you came out to see her every Tuesday and Thursday afternoon!" That hit Rossiter right between the eyes. His jaw went slack in shock. "You left on the next morning's ferry. I have a witness who saw you arrive that afternoon. She remembers the date because it ties in with something important in her life. Lila lied, and you backed her up."

"I didn't do a thing," Rossiter denied. "Okay, so I was sleeping with her. So I was with her that night. I didn't do anything to help her case. I was in California on business all during the trial."

"You abetted her!" Mark accused. "You could have saved me from that stretch in prison!"

Rossiter's breathing was labored. "What do you want me to do?" His eyes trailed to Mark's pocket.

"I want you to go with me to the district attorney's office in Riverhead in the morning. We'll leave on the first ferry."

"Okay," he agreed sullenly. "I'll meet you at the ferry."

"I'll pick you up," Mark told him. "And don't try to take the ferry out tonight because I'll be there watching. If you pull anything funny, I'll nail you for obstructing justice. Where are you staying?"

Rossiter gave Mark his address and hurried out into the night. Emotionally drained, Mark dropped onto the sofa. He'd have to be at the dock to make sure Rossiter didn't try to make a run for it.

"Mark—" He started at the sound of Anne's voice. She emerged into view. "I was out here with a tape recorder. It has a great microphone. I'm sure I've got everything he said on tape." Anne had anticipated his bringing Rossiter here. She'd remembered the tape recorder in the bedroom. They'd played around with it one night for laughs.

"A tape won't be admissible in court," he reminded, "but if Rossiter goes to the DA and gives him a story about coercion, we'll have the tape to back us up. That and Doris's testimony will go a long way." He felt a surge of exhilaration. "It's lucky you thought to rush over here ahead of us."

"Let's make a copy of this on my tape recorder." Anne was realistic. "It's too important to take any chance of losing it."

"Tonight," Mark confirmed. "But right now let's go back to the restaurant and let Doris know what's happening." He checked his watch. "A ferry just pulled out. Rossiter couldn't have made it. I'll be at the dock when the next one leaves. He won't get off the island tonight."

"Will you want Doris to go with you to the district attorney's office tomorrow?" Anne asked as they left the house.

"It should be enough to take Rossiter in. I scared the hell out of him." He smiled with dark humor. "I'm an ex-con. I might kill him." He wouldn't kill Clint Rossiter, his mind taunted—but he was arranging the execution of Tony Maglione. But how could he stop what he had already put into motion? He meant to stay alive.

"Tell me everything," Doris demanded as Mark and Anne seated themselves at the table.

Mark filled her in while his eyes watched Rossiter's girl,

fuming at the bar. Rossiter was too shaken to return. The girl was leaving now. Rossiter would have a lot of explaining to do.

At Doris's insistence Mark and Anne ordered the Black Forest cake and coffee. They talked in low tones about Mark's approach to the district attorney. The case would be reopened. He would be cleared. But this would be a hollow victory. Time was running out. He had to break with Anne.

"It won't matter that Lila's dead and can't testify again?" Doris asked.

"If she was alive, she would be open to prosecution for perjury," Mark said grimly. "And nobody can allege that Rossiter was paid to come forward. We tracked him down only because you gave us the lead." He checked his watch again. "I want to be at the dock when the next ferry pulls in, and I'll stay till it leaves. I'll be there again for the next one out. I must make sure Rossiter doesn't try to run."

"I'll go with you," Anne said.

"No." Mark was firm. "I don't expect any trouble, but I don't want you there in case it gets ugly."

"I'll take Hannibal home with me," she said. "We'll be waiting for you."

Chapter Twenty-Five

The alarm was seconds away from going off. Mark reached across Anne to silence it. He dressed swiftly—fighting yawns—and went out into the living room. Hannibal jumped down from the sofa in welcome.

"Okay, Hannibal, let's go." His voice was a whisper, but Hannibal responded.

They went out into the crisp, sea-drenched early morning air. He'd go back to the house, feed Hannibal, dress. Then he'd go over to the motel to pick up Rossiter. They'd be at the DA's office by the time the first secretary arrived.

He was running a full ten minutes ahead of schedule, Mark noted with approval as he prodded Hannibal out the front door of his house. Last night he had waited out the last ferry. Rossiter had not put in an appearance. In his pocket rested the copy of the tape Anne had made on her recorder. He had a witnessed statement from Doris, which she was prepared to back up in person. Everything was moving as planned.

Mark walked to the door of the motel unit where Rossiter said he was staying. He knocked briskly.

"Who the hell is that?" an irate male voice demanded. "You know what time it is?"

"Clint Rossiter?" Suddenly Mark was ice-cold.

"Damn it, no!" a voice called back. *Not Rossiter's voice.*

Rossiter had lied to him. It was too late to go chasing all over the community to track him down. The ferry! Catch the bastard at the ferry.

Mark charged towards the dock. Nobody had boarded the ferry yet. He waited. His eyes scanning the arriving passengers. No sign of Rossiter. The boat pulled away from the deck.

Rossiter had hired somebody with a boat to take him to the mainland last night! *Why hadn't he realized that could happen? Damn, he'd been stupid.*

Chapter Twenty-Six

Frustrated, furious with himself for overlooking this loop-hole, Mark went to a luncheonette for breakfast. He took no part in the repartee about the counter. His mind struggled to cope with the problem of picking up Rossiter's trail. He was mindful of the Vermont license and address. He had a name. He must work from there.

While he finished off pancakes and coffee, Mark plotted his next move. No time to castigate himself further for letting Rossiter slip through his fingers. Go back to the telephones. Try to locate a Clint Rossiter via telephone information in all the boroughs of New York. If Rossiter lived in Westchester or Long Island, then Anne and he would check every community. If Rossiter had an unlisted phone, he was out of luck.

Mark paid for his breakfast. While he waited for change, he dug out of his wallet the paper with the name of the PI he had been told about in the slammer. Jeremy Tyler. He had an office in mid-Manhattan. Tyler was supposed to be sharp. If he couldn't pin down Rossiter's address, then he'd put Tyler on Rossiter's trail.

Mark hurried to the phones. All were deserted this early in the morning. He dialed Manhattan information, tried for a phone number on Rossiter. If there was a number, all he'd have to do was look him up in the Manhattan directory, and he'd have the address.

"I'm sorry, there's no listing under that name," the operator reported.

"It may be a new listing. Would you check that, please?" He waited, conscious of his heart pounding against his ribs. *He shouldn't have let Rossiter out of his sight last night.*

"Sorry, sir. No listing under Clinton Rossiter," the operator said after a brief wait.

"Thank you, operator."

Borough by borough he tried to locate Rossiter. There was no listing anywhere. All right, start on Westchester. Town by town. But by the time he had gone through a dozen random towns in Westchester, Mark realized this was futile. He was being propelled by panic.

He checked his watch. Too early to try to reach Tyler. Go back to the house. Come here again in an hour. Call Tyler then. If Tyler was going to be in the office this afternoon, he would go into the city and lay the whole thing out for him.

Heading towards the house he spied Anne. She was so engrossed in thought she didn't see him until he called out to her.

"Mark—" She was startled. "I thought you were going to Riverhead with Rossiter."

"I lost him," Mark admitted. "He must have hired a private boat to take him off the island last night. I wasn't thinking straight. I should have stuck to him. Where are you headed?"

"The grocery, but it's not important. Come back to the house and we'll have breakfast."

"I ate at the luncheonette, but I'll have more coffee with you."

"What happens now?" Anne asked anxiously as they walked. "Can you take the tape to the district attorney?"

"I need Rossiter. I'm bringing in the private investigator I

179

told you about. It's too early to call his office. I'll only get his answering machine."

"Let's stop and bring Hannibal to my place."

"Sure."

How was he going to cut Anne out of his life? How was he going to tell her the whole truth? In prison all that had seen him through was the slow build-up of how to run his "hit factory" when he got out. That had triggered his mail-order degree, the sociology courses, his learning as much through law books as though he had sat daily in classes for three years.

At Anne's house Mark and Hannibal settled themselves on the deck. Anne went out to the kitchen to put up coffee. In forty minutes he would start phoning Tyler's office. He would try every half hour unless the answering service could tell him specifically when Tyler was due in.

Anne flipped on the stereo in the living room, then brought out coffee for them. Mark took a few gulps, then per plan went back to the phones to try Tyler's office.

"Jeremy Tyler's office." A friendly feminine voice answered.

"Is this the office or the service?" Mark asked.

"Service. Do you want to leave a message?"

"No message, thanks. Do you know when he'll be in?"

"If he's not tied up, he comes in around ten. That's when his secretary arrives."

"I'll try him at ten," Mark said and hung up.

He stopped at the newspaper store to pick up the *Times*, headed back to Anne's house. He'd have to sit it out until ten.

"Was Tyler in?" Anne leaned over the railing as he started up the walk to the steps.

"Not yet. I have to try again at ten." His head ached. The knowledge that he was being dishonest with Anne was unbearably oppressive.

They sat on the deck and watched a pair of sailboats in the distance, both conscious of each passing minute. Anne was anxious to help him relax. She pulled from her memory amusing moments of the two-week London-Paris tour she had taken with her roommate the summer she received her degree.

"Hi." A bright yellow beach cover-up over her swimsuit, Doris stood below. She was startled to see him here. "I knew you were awake, Anne. I heard the stereo."

"Rossiter skipped," Mark explained when Doris reached the deck. "I should have stuck with him."

"You have his name," Doris reminded. "You know he has a Vermont car registration."

"Mark's hiring a private investigator," Anne told her. "As soon as he can get a call through."

Doris dropped into a chaise.

"I've got news, too. My brother Ron is coming out here to-morrow. He's an attorney. When his wife died three years ago, he retired and bought a farm upstate. Now he finds he's going out of his mind away from the office. When he comes out here, we'll put him to work. You'll need a lawyer, Mark. And Ron's the best."

"He may not want to be drafted." Mark was uncomfortable. Everything was getting out of hand. Anne, Doris, and now her brother. None of them knowing the whole truth. They wanted to give him back his life, but it was in hock to Brooks. "Don't you think you ought to ask him?" Mark strived for a note of humor.

"He'll be delighted," Doris insisted. "I know Ron."

Mark left Doris and Anne to try to reach Tyler again. This time his secretary was in the office.

"Mr. Tyler will be in the office by noon," she reported. "He'll be here until two-thirty. Would you like to make an ap-pointment?"

"How about two o'clock?" Mark swiftly tabulated the time—he could be in the city by two. "How about two o'clock?"

"Two o'clock is fine. What name, please?"

Mark hesitated.

"Mark Cameron. I was recommended by a former client." A former client whom Tyler had helped clear of a murder rap, but who had been sent up later for extortion.

Mark checked the ferry schedule on the nearby bulletin board. He could make it by two with no sweat.

Doris had left by the time Mark returned. Approaching Anne's house he knew he couldn't let her go on thinking there was a future for them. The time had come to level with her.

"Did you reach Tyler?" she asked hopefully.

"Yes. I'm seeing him at his office at two." He took a deep breath. Gearing himself for what he must do. "Annie, come into the house. I have to talk to you."

"All right." She smiled but her eyes were anxious.

Anne walked into the living room, stood uncertainly in the center. Instinctively she knew what she was about to hear would be shattering.

"Sit down, Annie. I have to tell you something you're not going to like to hear." His face revealed his anguish.

"Tell me, Mark." She was pale.

"I went into prison with rage, Annie. The courts took away every chance of my following the life I'd planned for myself. I could never go to law school. I could never take the bar exams. You know what it's like for an ex-con on the outside." He felt fresh fury charge through him as he stood before her.

"Mark, you have every chance of being cleared now."

"You don't understand," he said with painful slowness. "My mind grew sick in prison. After the first year I looked for a way to fight back. And I found it." He paused, smote by recall. "I spent those next years plotting my revenge."

"Mark, I don't understand—"

"Those rotten punks you worry about," he said. "Those sociopaths who kill without remorse. I've set up a 'hit factory' using those kids. Because they can kill and the law will do nothing about it." She was staring at him with disbelief in her eyes. "Oh, I'm not accepting just any client," he continued with an ironic smile. "Only those belonging to the underworld. But for a price I eliminate people."

"Mark, I can't believe it," she whispered.

"As of Saturday you can believe it." He forced himself to go on. "On Saturday my first crew goes into operation." Her three kids that she'd talked about so much. Perez and Smith and Joey Devlin. But Joey would be pensioned off. He had sensed that Joey had been a bad choice. "It's all set up, Annie."

"Mark, you're not a murderer!"

"This hood deserves to die!" But his eyes showed his rejection of this rationale.

"It's not for you to judge. You don't want to do this," she said in sudden comprehension. "Maybe in prison your mind grew sick." She was fumbling for words. Trying to bring reality out of unreality. "But your mind isn't sick now. *You don't want to do this.*"

"No," he admitted. "I don't want to do it. But I've taken on a contract. Either I kill, or they'll kill me."

"Mark, I won't let you do this—" Anne rose to her feet.

"It's too late," he told her. "My timing was rotten. If I'd waited two weeks—"

"Let's talk about this," she pleaded. "We'll—"

"We could talk forever and it wouldn't change my deal. I'm sorry. I didn't want to do this to you." He forced himself to pull his gaze away from her and check his watch. "I have to go into the city to see Tyler. That's a big joke, isn't it? But I have to go through with it." He hesitated. "You won't tell Doris? You'll let her testify for me?"

"I won't say anything to anyone," Anne said passionately. "I can't believe this is happening. I can't believe any of it."

"I'm sorry, Annie."

Abruptly Mark strode from the house.

Chapter Twenty-Seven

From the ferry Mark went to the bank to cash a substantial check. Tyler would be skeptical about proceeding until a check had cleared. He left the bank, took a taxi to the Long Island station.

"I have to make a train," he said tersely. "Step on it!"

He made his train by seconds. Today the trip into Manhattan seemed intolerably long. The air-conditioning was ineffectual. His shirt clung wetly to his back. He was too distraught to read. He was on his feet and at the exit the moment the train went underground en route to Penn Station.

Tyler's office was in a building in the low Forties, off Fifth Avenue. Normally he would have walked. In the steaming heat of Manhattan he capitulated and took a taxi across town.

Jeremy Tyler worked out of a seedy building that indicated to Mark that his fees would be reasonable. His secretary—no more than twenty but bright-eyed and canny—was engrossed in a personal call when Mark walked into the reception area. She relinquished the phone and pushed aside the glass enclosure to greet him.

"Mark Cameron. I'm a little early."

"Sit down and cool off." She smiled good-humoredly. "Jeremy just went downstairs for a quick lunch."

Five minutes later Tyler arrived. Fortyish, neat, unobtrusive. He could easily lose himself in any crowd. A valuable trait for a PI. His secretary buzzed to unlock the door that allowed them inside. In this kind of building security was essential.

Inside Tyler's office Mark filled the investigator in on his background. He explained his need to locate Rossiter.

"All I want you to do is find him. I'll take it from there."

"This comes high," Tyler warned.

"I'll pay within reason. You ought to be able to pin him down fast with your connections."

They dickered for a few moments. Mark handed over cash. Tyler smiled in approval.

"You'll have to check with me," Tyler reminded. "You said you don't have a phone where I can reach you."

"I'll check in at five tomorrow," Mark said. "I'll check in at five every day till you catch up with him."

Mark left Tyler's office, headed back to Penn Station. He was beginning to feel like a yo-yo with this commuting between the island and Manhattan. Tomorrow, he told himself, he'd close up the house and come into New York.

He would have to go back to Annie's house to collect Hannibal. He dreaded coming face to face with her. She would be silent because she loved him. But she undoubtedly recoiled with the contempt she must feel for him.

On the train Mark tried to concentrate on a paperback he'd bought at the station. His mind refused to cooperate. Anne infiltrated his thoughts. Why was this happening to him? If he had never met Annie, he could see this through without pain. He could have played the gross charade he had worked out for himself.

On the ferry he remained on deck. He stared into the water without seeing. Hearing Anne's voice.

"Mark, I can't believe it."

Anne had brought him back to his senses. How had he allowed himself to conjure up this sick deal? He had come out of one prison to sentence himself to another.

As the boat approached the island, he gazed at the shore with fresh awareness. He had booted himself out of Annie's life. He would never come here again.

He was startled to see the drapes drawn tight across the front of Anne's house as he walked up the stairs. She never shut out the view of the sea. Had she packed up and left? But while he hesitated, he heard Hannibal barking.

Hannibal leapt up ecstatically as he walked into the living room. Anne was curled up in a corner of the sofa. She rose to her feet at the sight of Mark.

"I've been sitting here thinking about you all day." She crossed to confront him at close range. "I won't let you go through with this. You have a chance to live a normal life. We can't throw that away."

"I told you," he said tiredly. "If I don't go through with this contract, the man won't let me live. I've taken money from him."

"Send it back," she ordered. "We'll fly to Montreal. We'll live up there—"

"Do we need passports?" Mark was unsure. "I have mine—under Mark Cameron."

"And I have mine—it won't expire for years," she pounced in triumph. "We can leave tonight—without telling anybody. Not even Doris. Her brother's coming in tomorrow. Let him follow up on the business with Rossiter. But you'll be away from here. *Safe.*"

"You'd go with me?" He was captured by the prospect of leaving the nightmare behind him. *Can we swing it?*

"Of course I'll go with you. Arrange to get the money back to that man. But not until we're on a flight to Montreal. It can work! In Montreal you'll go to law school. Dad left me money, and I can get a job up there—"

Mark's mind catapulted into action. Annie was right. He could do it. He wasn't concerned about the punks. Give them five hundred each and tell them to get lost. But it would be rough to tell Chuck.

"I'll go into Manhattan tomorrow." Mark was decisive. "I'll arrange to send the money back by messenger. Not to be delivered until nine o'clock Saturday morning." In Montreal he couldn't be reached by Brooks. Nobody would know he was there. "Meet me in the city, Annie. We'll take a night flight to Montreal."

"But you'll have to talk with Doris's brother if he's going to handle the situation with the DA," Anne pinpointed.

"We have to be out of New York before the hit is supposed to come off—" Mark's mind raced. "It'll take split-second timing. But I can manage everything if I take an early ferry into the city tomorrow." Mark looked at his watch. "I can't reach Chuck. I'll have to call him later." Chuck expected a dry run tomorrow—but much later in the day.

Can this work? With no slip-ups it could work. He'd have to figure out every move. Anne and he must be out of the country before the money was delivered to Brooks. Hours before Maglione was scheduled to be hit.

Two messenger services, he plotted. The services were bonded—no problems about loss. One would deliver a locked attaché case presumably holding legal briefs. The other would deliver an envelope with the key. Brooks would understand.

He'd write off the kids with no sweat. Give Chuck a thousand of his own money and ship him out to San Francisco. Chuck always had a hankering to go west. He didn't want to think about the connections Chuck would make out there. But he couldn't run Chuck's life for him.

"I'll transfer funds for our use into travelers' checks in the morning," Mark told Anne. "When I pick up the money to be returned." He'd have to buy an attaché case, too. Brooks's case was in the back of the car.

Anne walked with him to the dock when it was time to call Chuck. Chuck was not there on the first try. Anne and he walked over to buy cups of frozen yogurt. To push away time.

In twenty minutes Mark returned to the phones. This time Chuck himself answered.

"Chuck, we have to talk," Mark said. "I want you to be at that pad you took me to that first time. Give me the address."

"Hey, Attorney, is somethin' wrong?" Chuck was uneasy.

"We can't talk over the phone. Give me the address."

Mark wrote down the street number. He was conscious of Chuck's anxiety.

"I'll meet you in front of the building at eleven sharp," Mark said. "Tell the kids to hang around the pool hall until we get there."

"Mark, we got the dry run set for tomorrow," Chuck reminded. A hard note sneaked into his voice. "Brooks tryin' to pull somethin' funny?"

"No," Mark denied. "See you at eleven."

Chapter Twenty-Eight

With an island-bought attaché case in tow, Mark left the next morning on the first ferry out. He was at the door of the bank by the time the bank guard was opening the front door.

He went through the routine of converting a sizeable amount of money from the joint savings account with his mother into travelers' checks. He left the checking account as it was. He could cash checks against it in Montreal later. He refused to consider that they might not make it to Montreal.

He went downstairs to the safe deposit box section. Inside the private cubicle he removed the money Brooks had given to him. He arranged it in the new case, locked the case. He pulled out the envelope he had brought along, Scotch-taped the key to a sheet of paper, and shoved this into the envelope.

At Penn Station he called Air Canada to make reservations for the last flight out for Montreal that evening. First-class, he reminded himself—so that Hannibal could travel with them. He shuddered, visualizing the cost of first-class seats—but Hannibal was part of the family now. He mustn't be stowed away in the luggage compartment.

Belatedly he realized this was summer and the beginning of a weekend. Would he be able to get seats? They could take a bus or Amtrak, but that would be agonizingly long. He waited anxiously for the reservation clerk to return to the line.

"Yes, sir, I can make the first-class reservations for you," the clerk confirmed. "Cancellations just came in."

"How late may I pick them up?" Mark asked.

"As late as one hour before flight time."

"Thank you." Flight time was 9:50 p.m. That was cutting it close, but they could make it. Somehow, making reservations for Mark Cameron made him feel as though he was returning to himself.

He checked the classified telephone directory for messenger services. He made five calls before he found two who were equipped to handle a specialized delivery all the way out to Long Island. Both open twenty-four hours, seven days a week. Expensive but necessary. Then he took a cab up to the South Bronx.

Chuck was sprawled on the stoop of the tenement. He jumped to his feet as Mark emerged from the cab with attaché case in hand.

"Jesus, I didn't sleep all night for worryin'," Chuck complained. "I kept tryin' to figure out what's goin' wrong."

"We'll talk upstairs."

"Okay." Chuck's eyes went icy cold. "Let's go."

The flat was empty. The two cots in the room beyond the kitchen were depositories for jumbled-together sheets and discarded clothing.

"Chuck, I have to give it to you straight." Mark strained to be detached. "The deal with Brooks is off."

"That son of a bitchin' bastard!" Chuck exploded. "He can't do that!" His face brightened in triumph. "But we got the first payment. We won't give that back."

"*I'm* calling it off." Mark's eyes met Chuck's without wavering. "Look, I went berserk in the slammer. I thought I could go through with this. I can't."

"We can't pull this on Brooks—" All at once Chuck was

Julie Ellis

terrified. "That fuckin' bastard will kill us!" He took a deep breath, changed tactics. "Mark, don't be an asshole. We've got a thing goin' that's worth millions of bucks, and nobody can touch us! We can't throw over somethin' like that."

"Chuck, it's out. I was playing a dangerous game with myself. In theory it sounds great—but I can't go through with it. I'm giving you a thousand in cash. Take a plane tonight for Frisco. You always talked about going there. I'm leaving for Mexico tonight," he fabricated.

"After all we planned?" Chuck was outraged. "I been workin' my ass off with them kids!"

"We'll send the money back to Brooks by private courier service." Mark ignored Chuck's rage. "In a locked attaché case. The key will go back by another service. Brooks will get the message. The deliveries will be made tomorrow morning—nine a.m. When we've left town," he emphasized.

"What makes you so sure you can handle these fancy arrangements?" Chuck challenged.

"You come with me." Chuck must see he wasn't trying to pull something on him. "For a high price you can arrange almost any kind of service." Even what they had offered Brooks. Mark reached into his wallet and peeled off ten one-hundred-dollar bills. "This'll set you up in Frisco."

Chuck was oddly silent. He was trying to digest what was happening, Mark surmised. At irregular intervals, as they walked over to the pool hall, Chuck's eyes settled on the attaché case containing Brooks's money.

"When do we go to these screwy messenger services?" Chuck's hostility was thinly veiled.

"As soon as we pay off the kids." Crazy ideas were swarming about in Chuck's mind, Mark guessed. He'd have to keep his eyes open. Maybe Chuck's sense of obligation to him was not as strong as he had believed—

192

They corralled the three kids into a deserted corner of the pool hall. Mark felt relief that Joey Devlin would not be taking a further step down the wrong road. Anne was right about Joey. He was a kid who could be diverted.

Mark handed each five hundred dollars and told them the deal was off.

"The cops are on to the whole show," he improvised.

"So what?" Frank Smith demanded. "We're ready to go to reform school. That ain't news to us."

"Yeah." Luis Perez exchanged an outraged glance with Frank. "Ain't that what this whole show's about?"

"You dumb schmucks," Mark whispered impatiently. "They'll catch you before you make a hit. You won't see a dime!" Perez and Smith were furious enough to kill him, he thought. Joey Devlin was relieved.

Mark and Chuck left the three in the pool hall, walked out into the sunlight. Mark scanned the area for a cab.

"What about the car?" Chuck asked.

"We'll take a cab down." He wasn't going to worry about the money he had invested in the car. Let Chuck make himself some deal on the street. If Chuck had any thoughts about grabbing the money, he wouldn't make an attempt in a cab.

They rode in stony silence the long route into Manhattan. Even this early, traffic in Manhattan was clogged. Finally the cab deposited them in front of their initial destination.

Mark was relieved that the building was a large one with heavily populated elevators. He distrusted Chuck's air of philosophical acceptance.

At the messenger service office Mark conferred with the manager, who was handling the special arrangements for the delivery of the attaché case containing the money. Mark emphasized that the delivery was to be made at nine sharp the following morning. Chuck could see this was on the level. Not a phony effort to cut him out.

In silence Chuck and he made the trip to the second delivery service. Mark completed the arrangements he had discussed on the phone that morning. It was over. The money was on its way back to Brooks.

"I knew you'd chicken out," Chuck said contemptuously when they were out on the sidewalk again. "Even that stretch in stir didn't do nothin' to change you. You were just a bullshit artist."

"Chuck, take that night flight," Mark urged. "Don't miss it."

"I won't." Chuck's eyes were chunks of steel. "I hope you rot in Mexico."

From Penn Station Mark phoned Jeremy Tyler's office to leave word that he had to leave town suddenly.

"Tell Jeremy my attorney will call him. He's handling everything for me while I'm away."

He didn't even know Ron's last name. He assumed Doris was right when she insisted that Ron would handle his case. But right now let him get back to the island.

Chapter Twenty-Nine

Anne zipped up her two valises that lay across the bed. Later she would worry about the apartment. She would write Chris from Montreal. He was a true friend. He would help.

She started at the sound of a knock on the door. Mark back this early? She darted from the bedroom to the front door. Doris stood there with a tall frosted glass in hand.

"Darling, Ron's here," she announced with a glow of pleasure. "Come over and have a drink. Leave a note for Mark to come over when he shows up here."

"I'll be right over," Anne promised. "I just have to put out fresh water for Hannibal."

She didn't want Doris to see the valises. How would they explain this abrupt departure? They would write from Montreal. Doris would understand. *Would her brother understand?*

Doris's brother, Ron Harmon, was a tall, slender, lean-faced man of about sixty. He had dark, penetrating eyes and a compassionate smile. While Doris prepared drinks, he listened attentively to Anne's recital of Mark's conviction. He stopped her at intervals to ask pertinent questions. She had brought along her tape recorder with the original tape.

"Shall I play the tape for you?"

"Please."

Listening to the tape, watching Ron's absorption, Anne knew they must level with him. Would Mark go along with that? He was sending the money back. Nothing had happened.

"Mark feels sure this investigator will be able to track down Rossiter," Anne said earnestly. "And he's convinced that with the tape and Doris's testimony, he'll be able to persuade Rossiter to go to the district attorney."

"Here's Mark," Doris said as he strode into the house. "Ron's here," she told him.

Doris introduced the two men. Anne searched Mark's face for some indication of reassurance. He appeared exhausted.

"I've been away from practice for two years," Ron warned with an air of apology.

"Ron, stop it," Doris commanded. "You're a damn good lawyer. That's what Mark needs."

"I don't know quite how to say this," Mark began somberly. "I have to leave the country." Anne was conscious of their shock. "It's a matter of survival. Not a criminal action."

"Why are you running?" Ron asked. Almost as though he was inquiring about the weather.

"It's better you don't know," Mark evaded.

"If I'm to help you, I have to know," Ron insisted.

"Mark, tell Ron," Anne urged. Still he hesitated. "You went through with everything the way you planned?"

"Yes," he acknowledged.

"Then tell Ron. You're in the clear. *Nothing has happened.*"

Mark turned to Ron.

"In prison I allowed my thinking to get messed up. I made insane plans." As succinctly as possible, yet unsparingly, Mark filled him in. "I have to run to stay alive."

"When are you leaving?" Doris was disturbed.

"Tonight. I've made reservations on the nine-fifty flight." He was careful not to name their destination. "Ron, will you take on the case of clearing me? Work with the private investigator? If I'm cleared, I can try to enroll in law school out of the country. I have funds," he emphasized awkwardly. Mom had put the money there for him to draw on as he needed. She'd understand.

"I'm not practicing for a fee." Ron was almost brusque. "I'm doing this because I think it has to be done. The courts have made a mistake."

"Mark, I haven't been able to buy a carrier for Hannibal." Anne was troubled.

Mark gazed at her in consternation. "I hadn't thought about that—"

"I think I know where I can borrow one," Doris said. "And when I don't return it, I can always order another sent out from Macy's to replace it." She put down her glass. "Stay here and talk with Ron. I'll chase after the carrier."

"We don't have much time," Mark reminded.

"I won't be long," Doris promised, charging towards the front door.

"We need to go to your place so you can pack," Anne told Mark. "Then we can pick up my luggage."

Mark turned to Ron. "We'll be right back—I don't have much—except my books. They'll have to stay here."

By the time Anne and Mark returned, Ron was finished preparing hearty salad plates from the contents of Doris's refrigerator. Doris had not yet come back with the carrier.

"Sit down and eat. I've become almost a gourmet cook at the farm. Almost," he stipulated.

"When does the ferry leave?" Anne asked, picked at her salad, anxious about making their flight.

Mark reached into his pocket for the schedule. "I thought it was later!" He took a deep breath. "It pulls out in eighteen minutes," he admitted in shock and Anne gasped. "Let's don't panic," he recovered quickly, his mind in high gear. "I'll cancel our plane reservations, ask for seats for tomorrow. We'll take an early ferry in the morning. We'll be off the island before the messengers deliver. Brooks won't know where to find me."

"Could we hire somebody with a boat to take us to the mainland?" Anne said in desperation. "That's what Rossiter did."

"We don't want to call attention to ourselves," Mark said, rejecting the notion. "We'll get seats on a plane in the morning," he decided. "We'll be out of here well before nine a.m." When Brooks would receive the attaché case with the money. "If need be, we'll fly somewhere else and transfer to another flight. We won't be where Brooks can reach me in the morning. I promise you, Anne—"

Chapter Thirty

Anne was in the shower. Mark left the bedroom, where his valise sat beside Anne's, and went into the kitchen to put up coffee. Hannibal trailed at his heels as though sensing the urgency of the morning. Neither he nor Anne had slept much last night—knowing they must be out of Brooks's reach before 9:00 a.m.

In twenty minutes they'd head for the ferry. By the time the messengers reached Brooks's place, they would be at JFK. They were picking up reservations on a morning flight to Montreal. First class. They were getting out.

All at once Hannibal was barking. He charged towards the front door. Doris, Mark surmised, with some last-minute advice.

"Hannibal, what's the matter with you? Knock it off."

He pulled the door wide and froze. One of the two hoods who had been with Brooks each time he was at the estate stood on the deck.

"Hold that runt," the hood told Mark belligerently. "I hate dogs."

"He won't bite." *What the hell is that creep doing here? Have the messenger services goofed and delivered early?* "Hannibal, sit!" Mark was in a cold sweat. *Let Anne stay in the shower.* "What are you doing here?" Mark demanded. Spar for time.

199

"Mr. Brooks sent me." The hood walked inside. Staring warily at Hannibal. "There's been a change in plans. We just got word at the last minute so I came out in the cabin cruiser."

"What change?" Because Brooks had received the money and knew the deal was off?

"Our man made different arrangements. He spent last night at his old lady's flat on Sullivan Street so he can drive her to the weddin'. From there they're goin' to his flat in Bay Ridge to pick up his family—"

"What's the address on Sullivan Street?" Mark interrupted. Play this cool.

"Here—" Brooks's emissary handed over a sheet of paper. "You know where he lives in Bay Ridge."

"I know."

"Brooks say he wants you should do the job before he goes to the church. He says, why spoil the weddin'?"

"All of a sudden, new plans," Mark said with a show of anger. Warning signals were jumping up in his mind.

"You're gettin' paid enough," the hood shot back. "Do it like Mr. Brooks says." All of a sudden he looked self-conscious. "Hey, if I decide to spend a couple of hours stretched out on the beach, nobody's gonna come up and ask questions, will they?"

"No," Mark said quickly. "Go straight down the path out front to the beach, then walk all the way down to the right. If you're in that area, nobody'll ask questions." *Away from the dock when Anne and I board the ferry.*

Mark stood at the door watching the hood swagger down towards the beach. He sighed with relief.

"Mark?" Anne appeared in the bedroom door. Wrapped in a towel. "Who was that?"

"Somebody asking about the beach," Mark improvised.

This wasn't some kind of crazy fix, was it? "Anne, keep an eye on the coffee, will you? I want to run down to the phones."

Mark dialed the messenger service scheduled to deliver the money. The office was open seven days a week, twenty-four hours a day.

Somebody at the service picked up on the third ring.

"My name is Mark Forrest." The name he'd given. "I left an attaché case with someone yesterday for delivery at nine this morning—"

"Mr. Forrest, you left it with me," the office manager interrupted. "Your man—the one who was with you—picked it up two hours later. He said you were nervous and had decided he should make the delivery personally last night. Is there anything wrong?" he asked anxiously.

"No," Mark said. "I just wanted to make sure he had picked it up."

Mark raced back to the house. His mind was in chaos. Chuck meant to go ahead with the hit on his own. Chuck was going to nail Maglione today. Unless *he* could reach Maglione first.

"Mark, what's wrong?" Anne asked with alarm when he appeared, pale and grim, at the entrance to the kitchen. "The ferry leaves in thirty-five minutes—"

"That son of a bitch Chuck. He's going ahead with the hit." Mark's voice trembled with frustration.

"Call the police! Tell them what's happening!"

"I can't do that to Chuck," Mark rejected. "I have to get there first and stop him." Chuck didn't know Maglione had slept overnight in New York. If he could catch Maglione at Sullivan Street, he could keep him from the wedding. Chuck would try to nail him either at his flat or coming out of the church. He wouldn't wait for the reception. Chuck was too impatient. "Annie, take Hannibal and go to Doris's house. Stay there."

"Mark, I'm scared." She reached out to him.

"Annie, please. Do as I say. I'll be back. *Don't worry.*"

Chapter Thirty-One

Mark arrived at the ferry moments before it pulled out. He remained on deck as usual, hunched over the railing, impatient to be in action. He'd have to rent a car. Christ, he had no driver's license! But he was loaded down with travelers' checks, which were as good as cash. Hire a car and driver. Play this by ear, with an eye on the clock.

He had plenty of time to catch up with Maglione if he could rent a car and driver right away. Chuck didn't know about the change in plans. But this was Saturday. Traffic would be heavy. Not that much time after all—

He watched for the sight of the mainland with painful urgency. He'd grab a taxi and go straight to the car rental place. Try to work out a deal for a driver. For money you could buy almost anything. But this was a summer weekend, his mind taunted. Pray they had an available car.

Mark was the first passenger off the ferry. He charged towards one of the waiting taxis. Knowing the drivers would want to pick up a full load.

"Look, I'm not going to the train. I want to go to a car rental place." He held up a twenty-dollar bill. "It's yours—"

"You pay, I'll go anywhere." The driver reached for the bill.

Mark stiffened into alertness.

"Is this your own cab?"

"That's right."

"I'll pay you two hundred dollars plus gas and tolls to chauffeur me for the next five hours," Mark stipulated. "I want to go into New York. Maybe out to Brooklyn from there. Interested?"

"Two hundred, in advance," the driver told him.

Mark pulled fifties from his wallet and handed them over.

"What's the first stop, Mac?"

"Sullivan Street in Manhattan. Know the area?"

"I grew up on Mulberry," he said with a grin. "Sullivan Street next stop. Name's Gene," he flung good-humoredly over one shoulder.

"I'm in a hurry," Mark prodded him. "Take the fastest route, but don't pick up any tickets."

Mark leaned back in the car. He was tense with the pressure of beating Chuck to Maglione. Gene was a good driver. They'd lose no time. Just let the traffic not be too heavy.

They turned onto Sagtikos State Parkway. The car was hot in the morning sun.

"What about your air-conditioning?" Mark asked, tugging at his shirt.

"It don't work too good," Gene apologized. "But let's give it a whirl."

Mark rolled up his windows. The air-conditioner was an antique. Hot air circulated about the car.

"Maybe I'd better switch off the air-conditioning," Gene said after a few minutes. "The car's overheating."

"Switch it off," Mark agreed. This car had to stay in working order.

They cut off onto the Long Island Expressway. The traffic was building up. Mark flinched each time they slowed down to a crawl. He didn't have time for traffic tie-ups.

Gene seemed to realize Mark was in no mood for conversation. He flipped on the radio, fiddled with the dial until he found a news program. They were making rotten time.

They left the Long Island Expressway for Grand Central Parkway. The sun was beating down in record heat. Mark's clothes clung to his body. His hair was moist with perspiration. Why did they keep running into these pockets of traffic?

They left Grand Central Parkway, crossed the Triboro Bridge, and headed down East River Drive. At Houston Street Gene cut off the drive and headed across town. Mark checked the address on Sullivan Street and gave it to Gene.

They made good time across town. In ten minutes Gene double-parked before the old walk-up building where Maglione's mother lived. Mark thrust open the door and charged towards the house.

"I can't park here," Gene yelled after him. "I'll circle around and come back."

Mark walked into the tiny foyer, read the names on the timeworn doorbell tabs. Here. Maglione. Third floor. He rang. Nobody replied. He rang again. Waited. His mouth was dry with anxiety.

Somebody was coming towards the door. A ten-year-old kid with a towel and swimming trunks under his arm. Mark grasped the doorknob as the boy emerged and moved into the hallway. The pungent aromas of food cooking somewhere on an upper floor permeated the halls.

Mark raced up the stairs to the Maglione apartment. He saw no doorbell. He knocked loudly. Nobody answered. Maglione and his mother must have left for Bay Ridge.

He waited impatiently at the curb for Gene to arrive in front of the house again. He glanced about for a 1992 white Coupe de Ville. That was what Maglione was supposed to be driving. No such car in sight.

"Bay Ridge," Mark said as Gene pulled up before him. "And let's don't waste time."

They drove along the Hudson to Brooklyn Battery Tunnel, through the tunnel onto the Belt Parkway. Mark fumed as they encountered heavy traffic again.

"What's that address?" Gene asked. "It's been a long time since I drove to that part of Brooklyn."

Mark repeated the address. He watched Gene's face in the rearview mirror. This was no time for them to get lost.

"Yeah." Gene brightened. "I know where it is. We get off two exits ahead."

They left the Belt Parkway. Mark saw a mixture of modest one-family houses and rows of decaying small apartment buildings. Here and there an apartment house showed signs of healthier incomed tenants. Mark watched the addresses.

"The next house," he said tersely. Inspecting the neat, well-maintained apartment building that sat well back from the street behind a patch of clipped lawn. The foundation was flanked by lush rhododendrons.

"Wait here," Mark ordered as Gene slid the car into a space just vacated by a delivery truck. Four spaces ahead he spotted a white Coupe de Ville. He squinted, trying to read the license plates. All at once his heart pounded. Maglione's car.

Mark left the taxi and hurried towards the house. Inside the small foyer he checked the doorbells. Maglione. Sixth floor. He pushed hard on Maglione's bell, moved forward to grab the knob of the inner door as someone buzzed from upstairs. He crossed the small lobby to the elevator. He rang and waited.

The elevator came to a noisy stop. The door slid open. Mark moved inside and pushed the sixth-floor button. His mind grappled with what he must say to Maglione.

Would Maglione have other hoods with him? Not at this house with the family to leave soon for a wedding, Mark surmised hopefully.

The elevator stopped. Mark walked out into the hall. He spied a door that was slightly cracked.

"What do you want?" Maglione called suspiciously.

"I have to talk to you," Mark said. "It's urgent."

Maglione scrutinized him for a moment, then moved out into the hall. He left the door ajar behind him.

"Okay, talk." He frowned as Mark gazed about uneasily. "Nobody's here!"

"Don't leave this house today," Mark said. His voice low. "I know you're marked for a hit. It could be when you leave this building. It could be when you arrive at the reception."

"Who the hell are you?" Automatically Maglione reached for his hip, then realized his holster had been discarded for the occasion.

"I hear things on the street," Mark improvised. "I don't believe in killing. I'm writing a book about the syndicates. I've been spending a lot of time on the street. The word got to me." Maglione was staring at him in disbelief. "Stay here, Maglione. Don't budge from your apartment today. It means your life."

"You know what I think? I think you're some kinda nut. Get the hell outta here before I call for the paddy wagon."

"You're set for a hit! Can't you understand that?" Mark demanded. "I came here to save your life!"

"I'll send you away in a straitjacket." Maglione pushed open the door to his apartment, walked inside and slammed the door behind him.

Mark heard an anxious feminine voice questioning Maglione in Italian. He couldn't understand Maglione's response, but the tone was derisive. That dumb arrogant hood didn't believe him.

Churning with frustration Mark went downstairs and returned to the car. Gene looked at him inquiringly.

"Let's sit here for a while," Mark said.

Gene stared at him in suspicion.

"There's not gonna be any trouble? I just got this heap paid off."

"No trouble. Let's just stay here."

"I'm thirsty," Gene complained after a few moments. "You mind if I go down the street to pick up a can of soda? I noticed a place."

"Go ahead, but make it fast."

"Want me to bring you a soda?"

"No."

Mark sat with his eyes galvanized by the entrance to the apartment building. He'd have to stick with Maglione until Chuck showed. He had to stop Chuck from making the hit. If Chuck killed Maglione, he would be an accomplice.

Mark saw the door open. Three elaborately dressed little girls were emerging with an air of conviviality. They ran in unison towards a car parked at the curb. A heavyset woman in a long flowered gown and elbow-length silver gloves followed them.

"Don't mess with the hedges," she called after the little girls. "Keep your hands clean."

The woman was halfway to the car with the little girls when Maglione emerged. At the same moment Mark spied Chuck rising from behind a hedge. He saw the gun in Chuck's hand.

"Maglione, get back into the house!" Mark yelled.

"Get the hell out of here," Maglione ordered, at the same instant that Chuck fired.

Maglione pulled a gun from his holster—the holster he

had not worn earlier—and fired at Chuck. He hit Chuck in the stomach. Chuck grimaced and fell to the ground. Maglione staggered two steps and fell. Mrs. Maglione screamed. She ran in her high-heeled sandals to where her husband lay.

"Tony! Oh, my God! Tony!"

Mark rushed to Chuck. He lay on his stomach. Mark was afraid to turn him over. Leave him this way until the ambulance arrived. He was unconscious. In bad shape.

"Somebody phone for an ambulance!" Mark called to the cluster of people who had suddenly appeared to gather around Maglione. "And the police!" He spun around to see Gene pulling out from the curb.

Neighbors hovered sympathetically about Maglione's hysterical wife. He was still breathing, a neighbor assured her. Mark doubted that he could last long. Other neighbors were spiriting away the three terrified little girls.

Mark stayed beside Chuck, sick at the sight of the blood that poured from the wound. Nobody came near.

A police car and an unmarked car with detectives arrived. The pair of police officers pushed back the horde of onlookers. The two detectives questioned the women who hovered about Mrs. Maglione.

"They were going to a wedding," one of the women explained. She shook her head in disbelief. "I was standing at a window watching the little girls go to the car. And then I heard a shot, and that guy there—" She pointed to Mark. "He yelled, 'Phone for an ambulance,' so I did."

"He shot first!" Mrs. Maglione said accusingly through her tears. "Tony was just defending himself!"

An ambulance pulled up as the detectives crossed to Chuck and Mark. Maglione was lifted onto a stretcher and carried to the ambulance.

"He's alive," Mark said as one of the detectives dropped to a crouch beside Chuck. At the ambulance Mrs. Maglione was being helped inside. "They'd better get him to the hospital fast!"

The attendants came over and lifted Chuck onto a stretcher. They carried him to the ambulance while Mark gave the detectives his name and address. Mark could hear Mrs. Maglione shriek in protest at Chuck's sharing the ambulance.

"You were a witness," the older of the detectives said and reached in his jacket for a notebook. "What happened?"

"I suspected he was going to hit Maglione. I rushed out here to try to stop it." He couldn't lie for Chuck and say that Maglione fired first. Maglione's wife was a witness. "I warned Maglione to stay holed up. He wouldn't believe me."

"Why didn't you call us?" the detective demanded. "That's our job. You'll have to come with us and answer some questions."

"First take me to the hospital to see if Chuck makes it," Mark bargained.

"That's where we're headed," the younger detective said brusquely. "If he's not going to make it, we want a statement before he kicks off."

Chapter Thirty-Two

Mark slid into the rear of the detectives' car. The older detective had introduced himself as Cassini and the younger as Weinstein. They shot out behind the siren-screaming ambulance. Cassini turned around to Mark.

"You know his phone number and next of kin?"

"No phone," Mark said. "He lives with his mother and a younger sister." Chuck's brother had OD'd four years ago. The nineteen-year-old sister had been a hooker since she was fourteen.

"We'll have a police car notify his family," Cassini said. He scrutinized Mark curiously. "You grow up in the same neighborhood with this guy?"

"We served time together," Mark said. It would come out soon enough. The cops were sure to run him through their computers. "I tried to stop the hit to keep him out of more trouble."

"Maglione's been in and out of trouble for years," Weinstein said. "He served time for numbers running maybe fourteen years ago. Then he moved into hard drugs. We could never pin him down. He must have got too big for his britches if somebody was out to hit him. Who gave out the contract?" he asked with calculated casualness.

"I didn't say it was a contract," Mark shot back.

With that hole in him it would be a miracle if Chuck made

it. If he did, he would be up for murder. How much would Chuck tell the cops? Damn, he had tried to stop the hit!

Guilt twisted knots deep in his stomach. Chuck got the bullet because he'd yelled out to Maglione. He didn't think Maglione had a gun on him.

The car pulled up in the parking area near the hospital's emergency entrance. Mrs. Maglione was being helped out of the ambulance. She was near hysteria again.

"Maglione must be DOA," Weinstein guessed.

"The doctor's got to make that statement," Cassini reminded, pushing open the car door.

The three men hurried into the emergency section. Every seat in the area was occupied. Attendants removed the two stretchers from the ambulance. Instantly all other activity in the emergency room was abandoned to handle the incoming cases. Shooting victims took priority.

A cop was uncomfortably trying to console Mrs. Maglione. He yelled to a nurse to see about sedating her.

"We're shorthanded," the nurse snapped. "This is the worst Saturday we've had in six months."

"Rosa!" Mrs. Maglione screamed as a festively gowned, rotund woman hurried towards her. "Rosa, they tried to kill my Tony!" She swung about to point at Mark. "He knew all about it! He came to the house to talk to Tony. I heard them talk about a hit!"

Mark flinched. He felt the eyes of the detectives dissecting him.

"Mrs. Maglione?" A nurse emerged from a room. Her eyes were compassionate. "Will you come with me?"

A moment later Mrs. Maglione's shrieks filled the air.

"They murdered him! They murdered my Tony!"

Tony Maglione was dead. Mark was involved in a murder. Weinstein was right. He should have gone to the cops.

Ten minutes later Chuck was wheeled out of one of the rooms. His eyes were closed. His skin paste-white.

"They're taking him upstairs. Let's go." Cassini charged towards the bank of elevators.

The two detectives and Mark took up temporary residence in the lounge area of the eighth floor. Weinstein left twice to make phone calls to the precinct. Mark sat tense and silent. His gaze moved compulsively at regular intervals to the door of the room where doctors worked over Chuck.

They waited almost two hours before the team of doctors emerged. Cassini and Weinstein moved forward with ID in hand.

"When can we talk to him?" Cassini asked the doctor who appeared to be in charge. "Is he going to make it?"

"He won't make it. If you want to talk to him, go in there fast."

Mark pushed in ahead, crossed to the bed where Chuck lay attached to lifesaving apparatus. His eyes were open. His breathing labored.

"Hey, I look like a character on TV, hunh?" Chuck struggled to grin. The nurse exchanged a glance with the detectives and left the room.

"Take it easy, Chuck," Mark urged.

"You gotta admit it, Attorney—it was a good try."

"Chuck, I didn't know he had a gun." Mark's voice was anguished. "I just wanted to stop you."

"Almost made it into the big time," Chuck whispered. "Fuckin' bad luck."

"Who hired you for the hit?" Weinstein asked.

"Did Maglione croak?"

"He's dead," Weinstein confirmed.

"Then Brooks owes me another hundred twenty-five grand—"

"Brooks?" Cassini pounced.

"Danny Schwartz," Weinstein said dryly. "He took himself a fancy name to match his fancy new neighborhood. You'll sign a statement?" he asked Chuck.

"Why should I do anything to help you son of a bitches? You ain't never done nothin' for me." Chuck began to cough. Blood oozed from his nostrils. The nurse, who must have been waiting outside, hurried into the room.

"You'll have to leave." She leaned over Chuck, reached for the buzzer.

Going out the door they collided with the approaching doctor. Down the hall a very young uniformed cop was walking towards Chuck's room with a short dumpy woman with over-bleached hair and a pantsuit designed for someone twenty-five years her junior. Her voice was raucous and profane.

"That fuckin' Chuck ain't never been no good since the day he was born. Always gettin' me into trouble. The bastard gave me that fifty-buck bill this morning, and then when I go shoppin', I get grabbed at Alexander's. I shoulda known if he gave it to me, somethin' was wrong with it!"

"Chuck's dead," Mark said coldly as Chuck's mother walked into the room. All at once he felt sick. From this woman Chuck had come into being. Maybe Annie was right. Maybe kids like Chuck were doomed from the start.

"What?" Chuck's mother stared in disbelief.

"There he is. Dead. You could have saved yourself the trouble of coming."

"Oh, my God!" All at once she was crying uncontrollably. The cop with her flushed. A nurse moved forward.

"We had her in custody," the young cop explained. "She was caught trying to pass a phony fifty. It was from that bank heist in Brooklyn ten days ago." Mark saw Cassini and

214

Weinstein exchange a loaded glance. "She said this guy Chuck took it out of a briefcase, which he locked up and told her to hold for him for a few days."

"Brooks paid off in hot money," Mark said tightly.

"How much do you know about this?" Cassini asked.

"Let's go somewhere and talk."

Chapter Thirty-Three

Mark sat across the desk from the lieutenant, with Cassini and Weinstein flanking him. A policewoman with a steno pad was recording his statement. Intent on supplying every detail, Mark spoke slowly. Starting with his frame by Lila Schrieber.

As Mark talked, he allowed part of his mind to try to cope with the problem of his own status in the present situation. He had withdrawn from the deal. He had tried to stop the hit. If Maglione had listened to him, he'd be alive.

"Look, did anybody at the scene know this Chuck Ryan?" the lieutenant probed.

"No," Mark said. "Nobody even came over to look at him."

"Okay. We'll play it this way," the lieutenant plotted. "We give the newspapers a story that Maglione was hit by an assailant whose name is being withheld—presumably because of his age. The son of a bitch won't rate more than a few lines anyway." He turned to Cassini. "Make it clear we're holding a kid, but we have to turn him over to Family Court." He leaned towards Mark. His eyes were sharply appraising. "When were you supposed to pick up the rest of the payoff?"

"I was to call Brooks after the hit and arrange it." Warning signals lighted in Mark's brain.

"Call Brooks and set it up." The lieutenant pushed the phone towards Mark.

Mark hesitated. He realized where the lieutenant was

heading. Then, in a cold sweat, he picked up the phone and dialed Brooks's number. The maid answered. Mark gave his name and told her the call was important. Brooks was at the pool, the maid told him. She'd have him call back.

"No," Mark rejected. "Take him a phone. You certainly have a cordless around the house."

Mark waited. The others watched him closely. They meant to send him in to collect, then close in for the kill. The rest of the payoff money was sure to be hot. It would work, provided Brooks didn't know about Chuck. About Chuck's mother going out to shop with a hot bill.

"Yeah?" Brooks's voice was guarded when he picked up the phone.

"Mark Forrest," he identified himself. "The delivery was made per schedule."

"How can I be sure?"

"Turn on TV or the radio—read the newspapers to-morrow morning. Call the funeral home," Mark said tersely. "I'll pick up the payment tomorrow at noon."

"Why can't it wait until Monday?" Brooks was cold.

"The deal was for immediate payment." Mark allowed anger to color his voice. "Tomorrow at noon is immediate."

"All right," Brooks said with a show of amusement, "but with a hundred twenty-five thousand in your hands, I didn't think another twenty-four hours would make any difference. You're giving me problems."

"You're not worried about going to the bank," Mark drawled. "I'll be there at noon. Have it ready." He put down the phone and turned to the lieutenant. "It's set up."

"Okay, you go in to collect," the lieutenant instructed. "It'll be more bills from that Brooklyn heist."

"I could be walking into a trap," Mark warned. "I might never come out of that house."

"You're taking a chance," the lieutenant acknowledged. "But if you carry this off, you clear yourself of any connection with the murder of Maglione. We'll make sure. We'll bring in the whole mob. You won't have to worry about repercussions."

"I told you I went into the slammer on a frame. If I'm going to gamble with my life tomorrow, I want a chance first to bring in the man who can clear me," Mark bargained.

"How do you figure on doing that?" The lieutenant appeared skeptical.

"I've got a PI tracking down a guy named Clint Rossiter. He was with Lila Schrieber when I was supposed to have been raping her. I cornered him once—I had a friend in the next room taping the whole conversation. He admitted he was with Lila that night. Then I lost him. Let me call the PI and see if he has anything." He looked at his watch. "I'm supposed to check each day at five. It's almost that now."

"Okay, call him," the lieutenant agreed.

Would Tyler be in his office at this hour on a hot Saturday afternoon? Yesterday he'd told Tyler he was going out of town, but Tyler expected Ron to call.

"Jeremy Tyler." A voice came over the phone.

"It's Mark, Jeremy. I've delayed my trip. Have you come up with an address?"

"Yeah," he said good-humoredly. Mark felt a surge of excitement. "This was an easy one. Got a pencil?"

"Go ahead." Mark reached for a pen and notepad.

Rossiter lived in a co-op on West End Avenue. Somewhere in the West Seventies, Mark estimated as he finished up the call with Tyler. A block or two from Mom's apartment.

"I've got his Manhattan address. He may be holed up there. Let me check it out." Mark waited for approval.

"Joe, go with him to talk to this Rossiter," the lieutenant said to Weinstein.

"We don't have a warrant," Weinstein pointed out.

"You're accompanying a material witness." The lieutenant shrugged, then focused on Mark. "This is your show. Threaten to go to the DA with the tape and your witness. That ought to loosen his mouth."

In Weinstein's unmarked car, Mark and he headed for Manhattan. They emerged from the Brooklyn Battery Tunnel and traveled onto West Street and up Saturday-idle Eleventh Avenue. Wasting not a minute. As they moved onto West End Avenue, Mark watched for house numbers.

"Here," Mark said. His mouth was dry with tension. Would Rossiter be here? Had he skipped to the country for the weekend? He had a Vermont address.

"I thought that on Saturdays in the summer all West Enders would be lolling at their beach houses or up in the country," Weinstein grumbled while he searched for a parking spot.

"Somebody's pulling out near the corner. The blue Buick."

He had a copy of the tape in his pocket. That ought to shake up Rossiter. What was that business about voice prints? Could Rossiter be positively identified that way? He searched his mind for what he had learned about sophisticated voice print equipment.

Mark and Weinstein left the car, walked into the small lobby of the apartment house. Mark scanned the doorbells. Rossiter, 8D. They walked to the elevator, rang, waited for it to descend.

The elevator reached the lobby. An elderly operator—an almost extinct breed—pushed the door wide. Weinstein held up his ID as he walked inside. The operator hesitated. He was probably supposed to announce all visitors.

"What floor?" he asked.

"Eight," Weinstein told him.

They rode up in silence. A lighted button on the board indicated someone on the tenth floor was waiting for the elevator. The elevator operator couldn't hang around to satisfy his curiosity.

There were only four apartments on each floor. Mark and Weinstein crossed to 8D. Mark pushed the bell. They could hear the chimes echoing inside. Mark felt perspiration popping out on his forehead.

"Who is it?" a male voice demanded from behind the door. Rossiter's.

"Mark Cameron. Open up. I've got a detective with me." Obligingly Weinstein held up his badge before the peephole.

"You got a warrant?" Rossiter asked.

"I've got a tape," Mark said with tight control. "My girlfriend was in the house when we had our little conversation. She taped every word we said."

There was a heavy pause. Then Rossiter pulled the door open. His gaze swung belligerently from Mark to Weinstein. He had been drinking.

"I don't believe you've got any fucking tape."

"Do you have a tape recorder?" Mark asked. Weinstein was staying in the background, but his presence upset Rossiter.

"Yeah, I got a recorder." Rossiter gestured for them to follow him across the foyer into the living room. "Go ahead," he jeered. "Let me hear the tape." He pointed towards a console that included a twenty-seven-inch color TV, stereo and tape deck.

Mark walked to the unit, slid the cartridge from his pocket and into position. He pushed the proper button, and voices filled the room. His mouth ajar in shock, Rossiter listened.

"Okay, so I was shacking up with her. So I was with her that night. I didn't—"

Livid, Rossiter charged forward to flip off the switch.

"Get the hell out of here!" A vein in his neck was distended. "That's not my voice. You can't prove it."

"Voice prints will prove it," Weinstein said. Unofficially.

"Doris Rainey, who lives next door to the Schrieber house, saw you on the island late that afternoon. She knows you were having an affair with Lila. She's ready to testify in court."

"Goddamnit! Why do you have to drag me into that mess?" Rossiter shouted. "I'm having enough trouble with my wife. She's up in our country house now with the kids— threatening me with a divorce. You drag me into this, I'm finished. Her old man will throw me out of the business."

"What about me?" Mark demanded. "You let Lila Schrieber put me behind bars for six years! You expect sympathy from me?"

"Look, Rossiter," Weinstein intervened, "you cooperate and this can probably be kept under wraps. The DA out in Riverhead will handle it with diplomacy. Your wife won't have to know. We'll work to keep it quiet—if you come forward on your own—"

"And if I don't?" Rossiter asked cagily.

"You'll be guilty of withholding evidence in a criminal case," Weinstein said. Rossiter grimaced. "Be good to yourself. Be at the district attorney's office in Riverhead on Monday morning."

"I don't have a choice, do I?" Rossiter seemed to sag. "You guys got me cornered. I'll have to play it your way." The effects of the alcohol he had consumed had worn off. He had an uptight wife and a father-in-law who held him in a financial pinch.

"The DA's office in Riverhead on Monday morning. Nine sharp," Weinstein said and turned to Mark. "Okay, let's go."

Mark and Weinstein left the apartment house and returned to the car.

"What happens now?" Mark asked.

"We'll hold you in protective custody tonight. You're a material witness. We'll have somebody pick up your car in the Bronx. You've got a set of keys on you?" Silently Mark pulled them from a pocket, handed them over. The car wouldn't be there. Chuck must have had it near the Maglione apartment.

Two hours later, from the lieutenant's office, Mark phoned Ron at Doris's house, briefed him on what had happened and what would happen.

"Don't tell Anne about tomorrow," Mark exhorted. "Just tell her to be with you at the DA's office on Monday morning."

"Right." Ron sounded calm, yet Mark knew he was anxious about the confrontation with Brooks. "She's here—I'll put her on."

"Thanks, Ron. Thanks for everything."

In a moment Anne's voice came to him.

"What's happening, Mark?" She tried not to show her alarm.

"I can't talk now. Ron will explain. Everything's going to be all right. You understand?"

"Did you stop Chuck?"

"I can't talk, Annie. Go with Ron to Riverhead on

Monday. Rossiter's talking to the DA. I'll be cleared of the rape charge." The lieutenant pantomimed instructions to end the phone conversation. "I have to go now."

Chapter Thirty-Four

In the protective custody of Weinstein and a uniformed cop, Mark settled in for the night in a pleasant hotel suite. The lieutenant was taking no chances. He wanted that collection made tomorrow. Officially Mark was being held as a material witness.

He slept in uneasy snatches through the night. He was aware that Weinstein and the cop alternated in grabbing rest on the other bed in the room. When he wasn't sleeping, he was staring into the darkness with his mind racing. How was he to handle the situation tomorrow?

Weinstein was scheduled to go with him in Chuck's place. That might alert Brooks, Mark considered apprehensively. They would have to play it cool, hope the switch didn't make waves. He had to see this through. It was his bridge to a whole new existence. His bridge to a life with Anne.

Not until traces of a gray dawn infiltrated the Venetian blinds did Mark fall into a heavy sleep. He came awake with Weinstein hovering over him.

"Okay, come alive," Weinstein said. "We've got breakfast waiting." He grinned. "It's not haute cuisine, but I think you'll manage."

"You've changed wardrobe." Mark grinned as he rose to his feet. Chuck would have approved of Weinstein's new outfit.

"I'm undercover," Weinstein reminded. "Do I fit the role?"

"Perfect casting." Mark was struggling to mask his tension. "Lead me to breakfast."

"They won't frisk us?" Weinstein asked as they walked into the sitting room.

"We were frisked at the gate," Mark recalled. "Not likely Brooks will order frisking this time. We're presumably in business together." The coffee was fragrant. He reached for it greedily. His stomach offered no welcome, however, to the scrambled eggs and toast. "But don't carry a piece, just in case," Mark warned. He gulped down the coffee. "Tastes great."

"They grind the beans themselves for every new Silex." Weinstein opened his shirt beneath the bizarre jacket to reveal minuscule equipment taped across his chest. "No piece, like you said. But I'm wired in case of trouble."

"They must be set up like an armory there," the cop remarked.

"We know Brooks's setup at the house," Weinstein told Mark, and Mark looked at him in surprise. "We figured he was involved in the series of bank heists that hit the five boroughs in the last two months, but we couldn't put a finger on him. We got a layout of the house from somebody who did some construction work inside. He's stashed his wife and two daughters there for the summer. He wants to keep a low profile when they're around. He has a man at the gate, two or three inside, and one patrolling the grounds. That's all for the present."

"Two inside," Mark confirmed. "I've had the pleasure."

"We've got a car downstairs," Weinstein reported. "We couldn't locate yours where you parked it in the Bronx. This one is the same model, same color as yours." He grinned at

Mark's astonishment. "We've got to keep the picture straight." He checked his watch. "Don't rush over breakfast. We've plenty of time. It's been drizzling since five. We shouldn't run into much traffic. Who wants to go to the beach on a day like this?"

They left the hotel, settled themselves in the car. Weinstein at the wheel. By the time they pulled away from the curb, the drizzle had stopped. Ten minutes later the sun was shining. Weinstein swore under his breath.

"All of a sudden half of the city's going to be on the LIE," he grumbled.

"We can go out on the Southern State," Mark pointed out.

"Any Sunday in July when it's sunny we'll hit traffic any-where. Let's hope nobody overheats. We've got this whole thing set up on a timetable with the local cops."

"We're damn early. Traffic can't mess us up too much." Mark tried to be optimistic.

The city streets were deserted, but by the time they hit the LIE traffic was building up. At regular intervals, as they sat stalled in traffic, Weinstein checked his watch and swore. This operation had to move on schedule.

Brooks couldn't know about Chuck. Not the way the cops were running the show. Unless somebody on the scene sized up the situation and got word through to Brooks. That was a long shot—but it could happen.

They were within a mile of Brooks's estate ten minutes ahead of schedule. Weinstein slowed down with a satisfied smile.

"That's our team," Weinstein said as they spied four un-marked cars parked at intervals at the side of the road flanking Brooks's estate. "It's up to us to go in and collect that hot money. Then they move in."

226

Weinstein turned in at the gate. Mark leaned forward to speak to the man on duty. The same creep as on the two previous occasions.

"We're expected," Mark said crisply.

"Who's he?" the hood demanded, staring hard at Weinstein. Making no move to open the gate.

"My associate," Mark said. He was beginning to sweat. "Look, Mr. Brooks is expecting us."

"Yeah, I know." Still surly, he moved forward to open the gate.

Weinstein drove through the gate and up the driveway.

"You in good condition?" Weinstein's voice was guarded.

"Peak." Like Weinstein, Mark was geared for trouble.

"We may have to fight our way out of here if that punk at the gate remembers me."

"Why should he?" All at once Mark's heart was pounding.

"I put him away eight years ago. For armed robbery."

"Inside the house—as far as I know—there're the two I met before and Brooks. They're big, the hoods that cover Brooks, but probably slow on their feet."

"If we smell trouble, we slug it out. The radio ought to bring help before too long."

"What's too long?" Mark asked with wry humor as Weinstein pulled up before the house.

"Before one or both of us gets plugged."

Mark touched the doorbell. Immediately the maid admitted them, led them to Brooks's office. Brooks sat behind his desk. A replica of the earlier attaché case sat before him. The same pair of burly hoods flanked him.

"Who's he?" Brooks demanded without preliminaries as Mark and Weinstein walked into the room.

"My other associate." Mark was cool. "I sent Ryan out of town on business."

"You delivered the merchandise?" Brooks questioned.

"You read the newspapers." Mark's eyes met his with a contrived air of confidence. "No hitches. Just like I promised. I have a date with a strip of beach down at St. Thomas. I'll be back in two weeks in case you have another assignment." Why in hell didn't Brooks hand over the money and let them out of here?

"You want to count the payment?" Brooks shoved the attaché case towards him.

"That's good business." Mark reached for the case. *Don't appear nervous. Don't be in a rush.*

The phone rang while Mark opened the case. Annoyed at this intrusion Brooks picked up the phone.

"Yeah?"

Mark began to count. He saw the sudden glint of steel in Brooks's eyes. The tightening of his jaw. For a split second his eyes collided with Weinstein's. Simultaneously they moved into action. Each took on one of the two hoods before guns could be pulled from shoulder holsters.

"You goddamn bastards!" Brooks yelled. "Cops!"

From the corner of his eye Mark saw Brooks rise from the desk and charge to the wall behind him. He shoved away the mounted swordfish. A safe was concealed behind it.

Mark and Weinstein punched frenziedly. They were out-weighed by at least thirty pounds each. The muscles were slow on their feet, but their punches were powerful. Mark staggered beneath a blow. He moved forward to crash his fist against the man's jaw. The muscle slumped—but as he did, he pulled a gun from his holster. Weinstein's foot swung up-ward, knocking the gun to the floor. Mark lunged for it.

"All right, on your feet!" Mark ordered. "Brooks, get away from that safe!" Weinstein had the other hood doubled up now.

Suddenly the room was overrun by strangers. The local cops were rushing into action. Weinstein relieved Mark of the gun.

"I guess the punk at the gate remembered me." Weinstein grinned. "On account of I look so much like Robert Redford."

At nine sharp Monday morning—with the sun beating down in record heat— Mark pulled into a parking spot before the large white Criminal Courts building in Riverhead. He sat still. His eyes were fastened to the building. Memories of his trial assaulted him. Anne silently reached for his hand.

Doris and Ron emerged from the rear seat.

"There's Rossiter!" Doris said and pointed.

Mark's gaze swung to a man striding from a car parked about sixty feel ahead.

"I didn't think he would be late for this appointment," Mark conceded.

He sat still for a moment with Anne's hand in his while they watched Rossiter walk towards the Criminal Courts building. Doris and Ron trailing behind him.

The nightmare was over. At last it was over.

Chapter Thirty-Five

Anne and Mark watched while Doris and Ron followed Rossiter into the Criminal Courts building, Doris as a witness, Ron as Mark's attorney. He was numb, Mark thought—he'd never truly expected this would happen. He was being given back his life!

"Let's drive to that restaurant Doris told us to go to," Anne said, her face exultant. "This will all take time. When everything's wrapped up, she and Ron will meet us there."

"I don't see how anything can go wrong now," Mark admitted.

"Nothing," Anne insisted. "Neither of us touched breakfast—let's go eat."

With Anne's head on his shoulder, Mark headed for the restaurant Doris had designated. They parked in the area behind the restaurant, walked inside.

"Thank God for air-conditioning," Anne murmured as they were wrapped in delicious coolness. "One of the great inventions of all time."

The regular breakfast crowd was thinning out. They settled themselves in a booth at the rear, ordered breakfast.

"We could have a long wait," Mark cautioned. His eyes tender as they rested on Anne.

"Whatever—" She reached across the table for his hand.

"Things should go the way Weinstein planned." Mark felt

a surge of anticipation. "It'll take a few days—maybe longer—but I'll be cleared."

Their waffles and coffee arrived. They ate without tasting. Nothing could go wrong now, Mark told himself for the dozenth time. Under the table his foot reached for Anne's.

"I'll have to phone my mother down in South America—if it goes through."

"It will," Anne insisted.

"Mom will be so thrilled. And she'll be dying to meet you, Annie. We'll have to wait to get married until she can fly up to be with us. It won't be legal," he joshed, "without Mom and my sisters there. Oh, did I bother to ask if you'll marry me?"

"You just did," Anne said softly, "and I said yes."

They'd finished off their waffles and two mugs of coffee by the time Doris and Ron strode into the restaurant.

"Please, God, let nothing have gone wrong," Anne whispered.

"What happened?" Mark demanded as Doris and Ron approached their booth. "Things went right?"

"Everything went right," Ron said, beaming. "It's a matter of a little time—but you'll be cleared of the rape charge."

Mark leapt to his feet. "I have to call my mother down in Rio and tell her! She's waited a long time to hear this—" He was fumbling in his pocket for change.

"It's South America—" Anne's laughter was shaky. "You'll need a bundle of change." Already she was digging into her purse. "Oh, what time is it down there?"

"It's just an hour later," Mark said, "but with daylight savings I'm not sure. But no matter what time, my mother will be happy to hear from me!"

With contributions from the other three, Mark headed for the phone booth in the far corner of the restaurant. His voice crackling with excitement, he spoke with an operator. Minutes later he heard a ringing in his mother's house. Then a pleasant, masculine voice.

"Hello—"

"Steve?" Mark asked. His bright, warm stepfather.

"Right."

"This is Mark—" They'd met once when his mother brought Steve to see him right after they were married. "Could I talk to Mom? I have something important to tell her—"

"Sure—" An edge of excitement in his voice. "Just a moment."

"Mark?" His mother sounded simultaneously excited and uneasy. "Are you all right?"

"Never better, Mom." Now he told her what had happened in the past few days, heard her sounds of joy as he talked. "I'll be cleared. I—I might even go to law school."

"You will go to law school!"

"And Mom, do you suppose you and Steve could fly up sometime soon? Just for a couple of days? It wouldn't seem legal for me to get married without you there."

He heard a startled silence for a moment. "Mark, someone you knew before—" Her voice trailed off.

"Somebody I met on Fire Island. Mom, you'll love Anne. She's a wonderful person." He managed a light chuckle. "When you two get together, I probably won't be able to get a word in anywhere. She's a social worker at a school in the South Bronx. You two will have a lot to talk about."

"Steve and I will fly up for the wedding." He heard tears in her voice. Tears of joy. "Don't you dare get married without me there!"

Three weeks later Anne and Mark were married on the beach at sunset—with Mark's mother and stepfather, his two sisters, their husbands and toddler offspring in attendance. Chris and his wife and children, Doris and Ron represented Anne's side of the family.

"It's like Shakespeare said," Doris declared at the wedding dinner at her favorite seafood restaurant. "All's well that ends well."

About the Author

Julie Ellis was born in Columbus, Georgia, moved to New York with her parents at high school graduation, attended drama school, was part of the early Off-Broadway scene as a young playwright and actress, performing by night, writing paperback originals by day, moving into hardcover with the million-copy bestseller *Eden* in 1975. Julie has published in fourteen countries, with many best-selling family sagas (*Publishers Weekly* called her "a master of the genre"), along with a number of romantic suspense, "cozies,", and contemporary novels that have received excellent reviews.